Cursed

Leigh Kenny

Sister Creep Press

Copyright © 2023 by Leigh Kenny

All rights reserved.

No part of this publication may be reproduced, distributed, or transmitted in any form or by any means, including photocopying, recording, or other electronic or mechanical methods, without the prior written permission of the publisher, except as permitted by U.S. copyright law. For permission requests, please contact the author.

The story, all names, characters, and incidents portrayed in this production are fictitious. No identification with actual persons (living or deceased), places, buildings, and products is intended or should be inferred.

Book Cover by Grim Poppy Design

Edited by Danielle Yeager, Hack & Slash Editing

First edition 2023

For Wig

To the world you are one person,

but to this person you are the world.

5

"By the pricking of my thumbs, something wicked this way comes."

William Shakespeare

"Welcome to my nightmare, I think you're gonna like it."

Alice Cooper

Prologue

The cherry-red glow of the cigarette reflected back at her from the window.

Staring anxiously out into the darkness, she took a deep drag and relished the sensation of it in her throat. She exhaled, smoke curling around her like an ethereal halo. Lowering her eyes, she flicked ash into the sink with trembling fingers.

Her body jerked back as something tapped the glass in front of her. Raising large brown eyes to the pane, her face contorted into a terrified grimace.

Two black holes stared back at her, a curtain of inky hair framing the void held within them. The thing's lips parted in a grin, stretching wider and wider until it seemed as though its face had split in two. It tapped again, its fingernail scratching gently on the glass. Speechless, she stared at the familiar horror before her. It tilted its head as it drank in the fear that marred her once beautiful face.

Without warning, it slammed its face into the window. A spiderweb of cracks appeared in the glass. Squeezing her eyes shut, she repeated the mantra she had held like a weapon for the past two weeks, "This isn't happening. This isn't real."

When she opened her eyes, the apparition was gone, but the tiny cracks remained. Proof that what she was experiencing was undeniably real.

Choking back a sob, she pulled a pink Post-it note from a stack on the kitchen table and with a shaking hand, in scrawling letters, she wrote, *For Cathy, I'm sorry*.

Tears flowed freely now as she stumbled up the wooden stairs and through the door to the guest bedroom, the note in one hand, a sharp knife hastily plucked from the butcher's block in the other.

The box sat on a floral bedspread, the one her grandmother had passed to her. Slapping the note onto the box, she quickly wiped her hands in revulsion. She made her way to the main bathroom, pulling the door closed behind her but not locking it. With the plug in the old cast iron tub, she rooted through the bottles and potions on the shelf. The orchid bubble bath was expensive, and she had always threatened to use it, but the right occasion had never seemed to present itself.

Well, no time like the present, she thought, emptying the contents into the streaming water. Steam wafted lazily, carrying with it the delicate floral fragrance, and with a deep, shuddering breath, she slowly peeled off her clothes and stepped into the tub. Her body dipped below the surface, the scented water easing the tension from her muscles.

A sudden scratching at the door flooded her with tension all over again, and she watched as the knob began to jiggle and turn. Without another thought, she lifted the knife from the floor by the tub and in one fluid motion, ran the blade vertically along her left arm, from wrist to elbow. She watched with curious detachment as blood flowed from the gaping wound, the water turning pink and then crimson. A sense of calm enveloped her, and as the light faded from her eyes, she slid deeper into a watery grave of her own making.

Chapter One

The sun beat down on the garbage truck as it traversed Main Street. Curtis pulled one hand from the safety rail on the back of the truck and wiped his brow.

"Sure is warm for April," he yelled to Tim, who was perched on the opposite end of the stinking maw.

Tim nodded, jumping from the back of the slowing vehicle and grabbing a can from the sidewalk.

Collecting on Main Street was the worst part of the job. Impatient drivers incessantly honking at the slow-moving garbage truck, having to sidestep pedestrians too glued to their phones to notice the men hefting the overflowing garbage cans, and worst of all, the cans themselves.

But the street and the town of Oak River looked great today.

The town committee had begun to decorate for the upcoming Spring Fling, a festival held in the small town every year. Nobody remembered quite how it started, but it had become an annual highlight for the residents. Even those who had long since moved away to start a new life elsewhere returned in droves for the annual Spring Fling. Bunting was strung around, and ladders still leaned precariously as the volunteers continued to hang flags and coloured lights along the main thoroughfare.

Main Street was awash with stores, most proudly displaying posters announcing the details for the Spring Fling. Little mom-and-pop outfits that sold almost everything on cluttered shelves. The laundromat that, oddly enough, played thumping techno music all the time. The First Family bank branch with its imposing façade. The record store that was run by a middle-aged white guy who tried so hard to emulate Bob Marley that it was embarrassing. The strange little curiosities shop that smelled strongly of incense and spices. And the restaurants.

So many restaurants.

For a small town, Oak River had more than its fair share of eateries. From the small, traditional family-run Italian restaurant, complete with red and white checkered tablecloths, to the numerous delis dotted along Main Street and elsewhere in the town. There were two Chinese restaurants and a small but vibrant Ethiopian café. Throw in a retro diner or two, a bakery, and a McDonald's, and you've got a small town with plenty of choices for hungry patrons.

All with garbage pails full of rotting food and leftovers scraped from plates. The cans from the eateries all lived in a constant state of stink, the miasma swarming with clouds of flies, buzzing lazily to and fro with no apparent direction.

Curtis and Tim worked their way along the street, diligently emptying cans as they went and hauling the empties back to their rightful places on the sidewalk. As usual, the small, exotic-looking man who owned the curiosity shop stood silently by his door, waiting.

Curtis didn't know why, but the man never left his garbage can on the street like everyone else. He seemed to watch for them, and once the truck began its slow crawl up the main drag, he'd appear, can in tow.

With a slow shuffle, the wizened old-timer would pull his can to the curb and then step back into the shadows of the shop's doorway, watching with eyes that appeared younger than the visage in which they were encased. Once the can was empty and the truck had trundled a little farther down the street, he would shuffle back out onto the pavement and collect his can, disappearing into the scented gloom of his shop until the following week's collection.

A curious little store and a curious little man, Curtis thought to himself with amusement.

The only upside to collection on Main Street was that it immediately preceded lunchtime, and wherever they chose to grab a meal, it was always on the house.

It was as though the proprietors along Main Street wanted to acknowledge the work of the garbage men, but only on that particular day of the week. Every other day, it was out of sight, out of mind.

It didn't bother Curtis, though. *I'll happily take the deal once a week*, he thought to himself, as he crammed another bite of juicy hamburger into his mouth and chewed.

Sitting in the shade beneath the awning of their favourite deli, Curtis and Tim chatted easily and murmured their appreciation of the unseasonably warm spring weather.

Sure, it wasn't great for hauling garbage bins, but now, feeling the soft kiss of a gentle breeze on his skin and listening to the musical chirping of birds and joyous laughter as kids and their families strolled along the street, Curtis could think of nothing more perfect.

Checking his watch, the worn leather strap barely holding together, he sighed and began gathering their wrappers, signalling a return to work.

"Back to the grindstone!" Tim said, cheerfully clapping him on the back.

Curtis chuckled and together, the two men stepped back into the sun, ready to complete another few hours of emptying trash cans.

As the day wore on, and with less than an hour left at work, Curtis let his mind wander.

He dreamed of that first beer he'd crack open the moment he got back home. The heat of the day was waning, but he knew the evening would be pleasantly warm, enough to warrant drinking a cold one on his balcony.

As he pulled a garbage can from the suburban sidewalk, a sudden movement caught his eye. A woman appeared from one of the houses carrying what looked like a cardboard box. As she drew near, Curtis could see the smudged eye makeup on her heavily lined face. She looked dishevelled, like she either hadn't slept in days or had recently been crying. Or both.

She stalked toward him on shaky legs and thrust the box at him.

It *was* a cardboard box, one just big enough to hold a household printer or something similar in size. There were symbols on the box, as though it had been stamped upon leaving some foreign country's postal system.

"Here," she said softly, barely more than a croak. "Can you take this thing away?"

Nodding, Curtis reached to take the box from her, but she snatched it back.

"Say you'll take it away. You have to *tell* me that you're going to take it!" she insisted, her voice breaking.

Curtis eyed the woman in bewilderment.

"Lady, is everything okay?" he asked, the concern evident on his face.

The woman let her eyes flutter closed for a brief moment, visibly collecting herself.

"I'm sorry," she said, the ghost of a smile on her lips. "I've had a shitty day. Would it be possible for you to take this box from me? It wouldn't fit in my trash can, so I'm hoping you could maybe toss it in the truck by hand?"

It was too close to finishing time for this.

"Take the damn box, Curt!" Tim yelled from the back of the truck. He was just as eager as anyone to get finished up. He needed to shower before he hit Broderick's Bar on Main for the game later.

With a sigh, Curtis held out his hands.

"Sure, lady, I'll take the box. No problem."

The woman thrust the box into his waiting hands and almost crumpled in relief. As she stepped back, away from the truck, she visibly brightened. She beamed at Curtis, touching a hand to her mouth as though she had forgotten how it felt to smile.

Before she turned away, their eyes locked, and Curtis could have sworn he saw a hint of something in her emerald eyes.

Guilt.

Fear.

Something.

Then she dropped her eyes and whirled on her feet, rushing back across the grass to her home.

Shaking his head, Curtis lifted the flaps of the box to see what was inside. People threw the strangest things away, and whatever was in the box, that lady wanted it gone real bad.

The box was empty.

Well, practically empty. Stuck to a piece of tape in the bottom of the box was a single, long black hair.

It didn't belong to the woman he'd just met; she had a bouncing mass of auburn curls. Curiosity sated, he shrugged and tossed the box into the back of the garbage truck to begin its journey to the town dump, along with all the other junk.

"What was all that about?" Tim shouted to him from the other side of the truck.

Curtis shrugged. "Beats me. Chick was strange."

"You seem to attract them strange," Tim said, braying with laughter. "Remember Lily?!"

"Lilah," he replied softly. "Lilah wasn't strange, she was awesome. That one is completely on me. I fucked up big time."

Curtis sighed.

He had dated Lilah for almost a year. She wasn't like any girl he had ever met. Confident in a quiet and unassuming way, crazy about the world and the wonderfully strange things in it, she had waltzed into his life unexpectedly. It was corny to say so, but she really was a breath of fresh air. However, she got tired of waiting for Curtis to decide what exactly she was to him.

He knew he could be immature and probably more than a little selfish, but he honestly never realised just how much that girl meant to him until she waltzed out of his life. It was too late by then though. He had come home from work one day, expecting her to still be wrapped up in his sheets from the night before, but her old, green Chevy was gone, and she with it. She changed her number, and last he heard from one of her friends, Lilah was driving around the country, living exactly the kind of free life she had always told Curtis she wanted to live, but with him by her side.

"Well, whatever about Lilah, *that* one is definitely not normal," Tim said, jerking his head in the direction the woman with the box had returned to.

Curtis snorted a laugh.

They shared a chuckle over the woman's odd behaviour and continued on with the last of their work. The weekend was calling to them both, howling at them like a wolf at the silver moon.

Chapter Two

A light breeze snaked around Curtis's bare feet as he reclined wearily in one of the plastic chairs on his balcony.

He reached behind himself, tugging the lumpy old cushion into a more comfortable position. His mind drifted to his earlier encounter with the oddly frantic woman in the leafy suburbs of Oak River. He could still see that glint of something akin to fear mixed with relief in her eyes as she passed that empty box to him. *Lord knows what her issue was*, he thought to himself. It certainly wasn't his problem. He just couldn't shake the strange encounter from his mind.

Swallowing deeply from his ice-cold bottle of Bud, Curtis looked out at the vista before him. His apartment was on the fourth floor of an old but well-maintained building not far from the centre of town. Through the leafy canopy he could see the tops of other buildings cresting through a sea of verdant greens. In the distance, the Oak River, for which the town was named, was visible only as a ribbon of silver, the evening sunshine glinting off the metal railings of the numerous bridges that spanned it.

Friday was his favourite day of the week.

Work was done, and endless possibilities stretched out before him. Granted, he did the same thing most weekends, but it was the bone-weary satisfaction Friday gave him that any kind of adventure could present itself to him. As if on cue, his phone buzzed on the table, drifting across the metal surface like a windswept leaf on a still pond. Curtis reached for it and swiped the text open, grinning as he read the content.

Draining his bottle, he stood and stretched his lean body. Curtis and the gym didn't agree with each other, but still being on the right side of youth and the physical work of hauling trash cans kept him in pretty great shape. He stepped back into his bright apartment, peeling his T-shirt from his frame and tossing it across the room and into the laundry hamper. Slam dunk!

Singing cheerily, Curtis busied himself with showering and dressing, ready to meet the guys at Broderick's for beers and a few games of pool. With a last glance back at the homely space that was all his, he palmed his keys from the hall table and pulled the door shut behind him with a smile.

Piercing rays of bright sunshine woke Curtis the next morning. He groaned and cursed himself for forgetting to close the blinds in his drunken state the previous night. Shielding his eyes from the harshest of the light, he lurched across the room and twisted the cord. With his thumping head temporarily soothed, he headed straight for the shower to try and wash away the worst of his alcohol-soaked fugue.

Curtis stood beneath the blast of steaming water, enjoying the sensation of calm it elicited. Movement beyond the glass doors caught his attention. A shadow was approaching the shower.

Curtis cursed himself for a second time that morning.

Had he brought a girl home and forgot? He didn't think he was that steamed last night!

He wiped at the clouded door and squinted through the distorted glass, but the shadow was no longer there. Sliding the partition across, Curtis stuck his head out into the room, clouds of vapor escaping and rising.

Nobody there.

Straining his ears, he heard nothing and dipped back into the shower, the warmth enveloping him with its welcoming embrace. He stood beneath the stream for another few minutes, mulling over the contents of his kitchen. Breakfast was always the best cure for his hangovers. He had it down to a fine art these days. Twisting the knob to stem the flow of water, Curtis turned to step from the shower and froze.

A single handprint was visible on the glass of the shower door, but not where he would expect one to be. The impression, small and delicate, like that of a woman, was evident on the lower portion of the glass.

A chill washed over him as he stared in disbelief at the print.

And then slapped a palm to his face and grinned.

Celia, the cleaning lady.

Celia came every Friday morning and let herself in with a spare key that Curtis had given her. She cleaned the place from top to bottom, retrieved her payment from its usual place on the kitchen counter, and left. Curtis was by no means a slob and always tidied up after himself, but having a cleaner once a week was a small luxury he afforded himself so that things never got out of hand. Celia cleaned things Curtis usually forgot to clean, like the window ledges, the oven. The shower.

Laughing at his own idiocy, Curtis dried himself off with a fresh towel from the hamper and pulled on a clean pair of sweatpants. His rumbling stomach pulled him to the kitchen in search of food. A quick glance in the refrigerator and his mind was made up. Eggs with a side of buttery toast would be perfect. He pulled what he needed from the shelves and set about whisking eggs and pouring them into a pan to cook. Stepping across to the far side of the kitchen, he tossed the empty shells into the trash and then widened his eyes.

There on the floor, resting innocuously next to the garbage can, was a box.

An ordinary cardboard box.

With strange letters and symbols on its side.

"What in the hell is this?" he said aloud to his empty kitchen.

A sizzle from the stove drew his attention, and he rushed to save his eggs.

As he finished preparing his food, he thought about the appearance of the box. As he sat at the small dining nook by the window, eating his meal and listening to the birds sing in the huge oak trees out back, he thought about the box. He glanced uneasily across the kitchen every now and then, as though the inanimate object would suddenly grow legs and charge at him.

It's just a box, he thought to himself. He didn't know why it was making him so uneasy.

His phone buzzed, startling him. It was Tim.

"Hey, asshole," Curtis greeted him. "Did you leave that dirty dumpster box in my apartment?" His eyes flicked to the box once more.

"Morning, princess," replied Tim with a chuckle. "I have no goddamn idea what you're talking about. Are you still wasted?"

Curtis huffed in annoyance.

"No, dickhead, I'm not wasted. I got up to make breakfast and the stupid box from work is in my kitchen. The one that weird lady wanted us to take away."

"Beats me," said Tim. "I'll be over in thirty to pick you up. And before you ask why or make excuses, you promised last night. It can be your good deed for the day. Or month. Your choice, buddy."

Before Curtis could protest, the phone beeped, and Tim was gone.

He groaned, running his hands through his hair, the dark locks spiking in their wake. He hadn't forgotten. He had promised Tim last night in Broderick's that he'd help him out in his elderly aunt's garden today. It was nothing major, a little clipping and trimming, mowing the lawn, but now, in the cold light of day and with a thumping headache hammering his skull, the last thing Curtis wanted to do was spend hours in the heat.

Sighing, he stood and slid his dishes into the sink. The warm spring sun continued to beat down outside. That heat would probably sweat the hangover right out of him. He cast another uneasy glance at the cardboard box before disappearing back into his bedroom to prepare for the day ahead.

The dim glow of the TV bathed the living room in soft blue light. Curtis reclined across his couch, his body almost disappearing into the deep cushions. What little energy he'd had today was completely zapped by the time Tim dropped him back home a few hours earlier. He had made a beeline for the shower to cleanse his sweat-soaked body and then fell face-first onto his bed and was asleep in seconds. He had come to a short while ago and dragged his weary body from the bed to the couch, flicked on the TV, and perused a few takeout menus before settling on pizza. Some mindless action movie droned on above him on the screen, but his mind was elsewhere.

He couldn't shake the feeling of unease that had crept over him ever since he'd seen the cardboard box in his kitchen that morning.

He had asked Tim about it again as soon as he had heaved himself into the truck. Tim was adamant that he had nothing to do with its appearance, then broke into a huge grin. Thinking his friend was about to admit to the prank, Curtis was thrown when Tim cried, "Who is she? Who's the lucky girl??"

Curtis had looked at him dumbly.

"Who is who?" he had asked.

"The girl, Casanova," Tim had replied, still grinning maniacally. "You obviously brought someone home from Broderick's last night. Don't be shy. Share the details, my man. Let a married man live vicariously through you!"

Still confused, Curtis had stammered about not bringing anybody home last night, but for a moment, his mind had flashed back to his shower that morning and the same assumption he had made.

"Well, who does this belong to then?" asked Tim, reaching across and peeling a long black strand from Curtis's T-shirt. "Sure as shit isn't yours, lover boy." Tim howled a laugh, amused by his own commentary.

Curtis's eyes had widened as he plucked the hair from his friend's fingers. Without another word, he held his hand out the truck window and let the obsidian strand float away on the breeze.

Tim had ribbed him for a little longer, but he realised soon enough that it was bothering Curtis. It irked Curtis enough that he couldn't bring himself to mention the box anymore.

He cast his eyes again toward the kitchen.

He hadn't been in there since he had returned home, but he assumed the damn box was still there.

Unless he had imagined it this morning.

Knowing that it would continue to dominate his mind until he did something about it one way or another, Curtis dragged himself from the sofa with a deep sigh. As he reached the threshold of the kitchen, an icy prickle danced along his scalp. Without any further thought, he reached around the corner and slapped his open palm against the light switch, banishing the shadows as the room instantly flooded with bright light.

He hadn't imagined it.

The cardboard box was still nestled on the floor by the trash can.

"Why am I making such a big deal out of this?" he asked himself, irritated at how much dominion he was giving to a stupid, inanimate object.

"Enough is enough." With gritted teeth, he marched across the room and grasped the box.

Flinging his apartment door wide, he jogged down four flights of stairs, gripping the box as though it would float away if he lessened his hold on it. He stalked out into the night and around the corner of the building to where the communal dumpsters were stationed. Pulling the heavy lid up on the closest receptacle, he dumped the box inside and dropped the lid with an unceremonious clatter.

A sudden, sharp intake of breath hissed slowly in his ear. Curtis froze.

His whole body felt as though it had been doused in ice water and his nerves stood to attention. With a heavy gulp, he spun around to face whoever stood by his shoulder.

Nobody.

The parking lot was a ghost town.

Without another thought, Curtis turned and ran back toward the building, hammering the elevator call button as soon as he reached the lobby. As the elevator made its slow descent toward him, he spun and weaved on his feet like a prized boxer anticipating an attack. The doors slid open with a mechanical whirr, and Curtis practically dived into the compartment in relief. He hit the button for the fourth floor, staring through the slowly closing doors to ensure nobody could sneak up behind him. Once the doors closed, Curtis dropped to the floor in relief. He crossed his legs and stayed on the thin carpet of the elevator floor as it rose through the building, letting his heart rate slow down. He trained his eyes on the numbered buttons as they lit up in sequence. Then with a jolt, Curtis cried out, staggering to his feet.

He had felt something brush the back of his neck as he sat there.

Like a mane of long hair gently sweeping along the top of his spine. Curtis scanned the small interior, his breath spilling from him in ragged bursts. There was nobody there. He *knew* there was nobody there. Had watched the doors close on an elevator compartment that contained nobody else but him only moments ago.

He didn't *feel* alone though.

With a ding announcing his destination, the doors whirred open, spilling Curtis out onto the carpeted hallway of the fourth floor. He stayed on the floor, watching with wild eyes until the doors finally closed once again on the empty compartment.

Dragging himself from the ground, he lurched toward his open apartment door, slamming it once he was inside. He stood with his back to the wooden door, catching his breath.

There was a gentle knock on the door.

Curtis leaned toward the spyhole on the door and held his breath.

The hallway was empty. Nothing but maroon carpet and dusty pink walls.

He slowly stepped back from the door and stood motionless.

BANG! BANG!

Something began to pound on the door. With ever-widening eyes, Curtis could see the door bounce slightly in its frame against the onslaught of whatever was on the other side.

Chapter Three

*B*ANG! BANG!

"Go away!" Curtis moaned in fright, and as though heeding his request, the banging ceased.

Curtis ran a trembling hand through his hair, eyes darting around him.

Tap. Tap.

Gentle knocking now, but this time Curtis staggered forward, intending to confront his assailant.

"I said, GO AWAY!!" he roared as he swung the door open.

A freckle-faced kid stood there, steaming pizza box in hand. The kid looked terrified.

Silently berating himself for being such a fool, Curtis took the food and tipped the kid a handsome sum in exchange for his silence on the matter. Told him that some kids in the building had been playing ding-dong-ditch and apologised profusely. The kid, probably relieved that he hadn't just delivered to an actual crazy person, gave him an easy grin and a wink of understanding.

"No worries, pal," he said, "happens to the best of us."

And with that, the kid sauntered back to the elevator, his pocket bulging with a tip that was probably more than his nightly wage.

With an exasperated sigh, Curtis dropped heavily onto the sofa and hit PLAY on the remote. The room came alive again with the sounds of excitement and gunfire. No matter who came knocking, he wasn't moving from his spot. Other than to replace his beers as needed.

As he watched the movie, chewing on a cheesy slice of perfection, he found his eyes drifting back toward the door on occasion.

It didn't knock again.

Lilah climbed across him, draping her small frame over his. He could feel the delicate strands of her long blonde hair that had fallen over his face. Even with his eyes closed, he knew she was watching him while he slept, could feel the intensity of her burning gaze. With a small smile tugging at his lips, he reached an arm out to encircle her, to pull her closer.

Her skin was so cold.

He tried to pull her tighter to his chest to share his body heat, but with the agility of a feline, she extricated herself from his grasp and padded away almost silently.

Curtis's eyes shot open, his heart hammering in his chest.

Lilah was long gone, yet it had felt more tangible than any dream he'd ever had. He pulled himself up from where he lay on the sofa, having fallen asleep during the movie. The screen on the TV was bouncing from one recommended Netflix title to the next. Wiping drool from his stubble, Curtis stilled suddenly.

It sounded like someone was rustling around in the kitchen.

His mind was in a jumble, walking a tightrope between the dream-world and reality. He could still recall with perfect clarity the feeling of a body meshing with his own and the chill of the skin he touched.

More rustling sounds travelled from the next room.

Curtis stood and stepped as silently as he could toward the kitchen. He stopped just beyond the doorway and pulled a deep breath into his lungs. Then he quickly stepped around the corner and into the room. A flap on the cardboard box moved slightly, then stilled as he entered.

The box.

Curtis stared in disbelief at the offending container, now nestled near the dining nook by the window. Moonlight streamed through the glass, illuminating the strange symbols that were taped to the box.

How did it get in here? he thought to himself frantically. *What the fuck is going on?*

Moving closer to it, Curtis could see strands of dark hair protruding from the unsealed flaps. He closed his eyes, swallowing heavily.

Another rustling sound, this time much closer.

Eyes springing open in panic, Curtis saw nothing. Even the wisps on the box were gone. But the moonlight had changed, so they were probably a figment of his imagination to begin with.

Or so he told himself.

He backed out of the room, his eyes never leaving the box. Flicking off the TV, he double-checked all the locks before heading straight to his bedroom.

Curtis sat on the unmade bed, his head in his hands. He had no idea what was going on, and he had no idea how the box had reappeared in his kitchen. Feeling a tickle at his chest, he reached toward his collar and dislodged the irritation. A horrified moan escaped his lips as he brought his hand up to his face. Another long, raven-black hair was laced around his fingers. It was a weightless and delicate thing but had all the impact of a noose pulled tight around his neck.

Curtis stepped across to the wastepaper basket and dropped the hair. It floated downwards, his stomach tightening as he watched its slow descent. For the first time in his adult life, Curtis closed his bedroom door and clicked the lock into place.

He stripped off his clothes and lay in bed, the covers bunched tightly in his fists. His mind raced in a thousand different directions as he thought about the box and all of the strange occurrences that had happened since that morning.

"This shit doesn't happen in real life," he said aloud in the darkness.

As though in answer, a frantic scratching began tearing at his bedroom door. Bolting upright in his bed, Curtis looked in horrified fascination at the shadows that danced within the crack of light beneath the door. Squeezing his eyes shut so tightly that he half expected his eyeballs to disappear into the back of his skull, he prayed to many gods, none of whom he believed in. He prayed feverishly. Words that weren't even prayers but on the desperate tongue of a broken man sounded suspiciously like supplication.

Realizing that silence had once again descended on his home, Curtis braved opening one eye. Then both.

The scratching had stopped, and the shadows were gone. The space beneath the door was once again a solid strip of light. Breathing a shaky sigh of relief, Curtis lay down and pulled the heavy blanket over his head. As the adrenaline drained from his body, he felt a wave of exhaustion roll over him. It didn't take long for him to fall into a deep sleep, but it was not a restful one. Thoughts of the box followed Curtis into his dreams, and he spent the night in a fitful sleep, one filled with a Stygian darkness that housed untold horrors.

With trembling hands, Curtis clasped the mug of steaming coffee to his chest. His eyes darted around nervously, like those of an animal that knew it was being hunted. They came to rest once more on the box.

Monday morning had rolled around, and unlike his usual unenthusiastic demeanour, Curtis was itching to get out of the apartment. Even if it meant work.

The previous day had been like a waking nightmare for him. He shuddered, thinking about it.

After waking up Sunday morning in a panicky sweat, sheets twisting and constricting around his body, like hands trying to pull him into some infernal abyss, he was suddenly frozen in place upon seeing his bedroom door wide open. *Did I lock it properly?* he had thought to himself, knowing deep down that he most definitely had.

With a fleeting courage instilled in him by the last tendrils of sleep, he marched out to the kitchen, lifted the box from its resting place and tossed it out through his apartment door and into the gloomy hallway. He watched as it skidded along the carpet before coming to a rest halfway down the hall. It never once tumbled or flipped as one would expect of an empty cardboard box thrown with great force.

Slamming the door and flipping the locks into place once more, he leaned against the door and exhaled heavily. Fearing a repeat of the banging incident from the previous evening, he quickly moved away from the door and headed for the shower.

The water soothed much of the aching tension from his limbs, and as he stepped out from the cubicle and wrapped a towel around his waist, he felt a million times better. Standing at the wash basin brushing his teeth, his skin began to crawl as he looked in the mirror and noticed the reflection of the shower behind him. He hadn't noticed until it was in his direct line of sight, but could now clearly see a multitude of handprints pressed into the glass. At least a dozen. Curtis glanced around the small room uneasily before dropping his toothbrush in the sink and stalking from the room, shutting the door firmly behind him.

"Keep yourself busy," he said aloud to himself, as he began tugging the covers and sheets from his bed. "Don't overthink it or your brain is going to break."

As he had pulled the unused pillow from the opposite side to where he usually slept, Curtis recoiled in horror. Strands of dark hair were stuck to the pillow cover, like the seedy reminder of a one-night stand that never happened.

With closed eyes and gritted teeth, he had finished stripping his bed before tossing everything in a pile. Every Sunday, he headed to the laundry section in the building's basement to keep up with his washing. It was as much a part of his routine as showers and shaving. Toting the bundle of sheets and clothes, he added them to the laundry hamper in the hallway before heading to the kitchen for coffee.

Curtis stopped dead at the end of the hall, directly between the kitchen and living room, for there, perched upon the welcome mat inside his front door, was the box.

In disbelief and without a second thought, he grabbed it for the second time that morning and crossed the living room.

He flipped the lock and pulled open the sliding glass door to the balcony, and while shielding his eyes from the early morning sun with one hand, he tossed the box out across the railing. Without even checking to see where it landed, he stepped back inside and slid the door closed behind him, clicking the lock into place once more.

In any normal situation, Curtis would never dream of littering—he was a garbage man, for chrissakes—but this was no normal situation. This was an utterly ridiculous situation. The kind idiotic jocks and their big-breasted girlfriends got themselves into in every Hollywood horror movie.

"Jesus Christ," Curtis said, pulling his hands across his face.

He headed back to the kitchen, glancing around himself surreptitiously, but the box was nowhere to be seen.

For now.

With a giant mug of coffee in one hand and a couple of cinnamon rolls in the other, he stretched out on the couch.

He had stayed there for most of the day, watching mindless TV and eating junk, moving only to run to the basement and throw his clothes in the washer and then again to transfer them to the dryer. The residents weren't supposed to leave their belongings unattended, but nobody paid any attention to the numerous signs plastered around the laundry room.

As the last light of the day began to wane, he knew it was time to rouse himself and head downstairs to collect his linens and clothing from the big industrial tumble dryer. With a sigh, he heaved himself off the sofa, stuck his feet into his sliders, and headed out the door, grabbing the empty laundry basket as he went.

When the elevator doors opened, Mrs Mathers from one of the fifth-floor apartments was already in the compartment, two small fluffy dogs attached by leashes to her wrist.

Curtis smiled warmly at her, and the two chatted easily until she disembarked on the ground floor. As the elevator doors slid shut behind her, ready to continue its descent to the basement level, Curtis noticed a tiny pool of urine seeping into the carpet. He grinned, knowing that the rented apartments, like the one the old lady lived in, didn't allow pets. He made a mental note to clean the stain after he collected his laundry, just in case anybody else happened to see it and report the woman. She was a nice person, and her dogs were quiet, not at all snappy like most of the small canines he encountered.

Mrs Mathers occasionally invited Curtis up for coffee or brought casseroles to his door. She was easy to get along with.

"Call me Helena," she always said in a playfully scolding tone, but each time he met her, Curtis found himself reverting right back to her formal title. It was how his Gramma Tessa had raised him.

The elevator doors whirred open, and Curtis strolled through the basement, his footsteps echoing off the concrete floor. He passed rows of cages, each belonging to a different resident or apartment owner, until he reached the small room that housed the washers and dryers. He pulled his items from the machine, haphazardly folding as he went, then he flicked off the machines and the lights to the room and headed back to the elevator. He hit the call button, but nothing happened. There were no lights on the panel or on the floor numbers listed above the metal doors.

"Shit!" he exclaimed, "The universe has a real hard-on for me this weekend."

Heading around the corner to the stairwell door, he pushed it open and glanced up. The stairwell from the basement was different than the main one in the building. The open stairway ran from the ground floor right up to the fifth floor, but the stairs from the basement were internally hidden behind a multitude of doors, all marked with a fire exit sign. Why the building had two sets of stairs, he didn't know. He only knew that he *hated* taking the basement stairs.

It was a concrete tomb filled with shadows and echoes, the overhead lights on sensors so that the place remained in total darkness, except for the section you were traversing. It was creepy as shit at the best of times, and after the weekend he'd had so far, it was an absolute nightmare.

But he had little choice.

Stay in the creepy basement until God knows when or take the creepy stairs and get back to the comfort and safety of his light-filled apartment.

Steeling himself, Curtis stepped through the doorway.

The overhead lights buzzed to life above him. He hauled himself up the cold, hard steps, basket tucked under his arm, trying not to think about anything other than focusing on each step he took. The light behind him clicked off as the new one above him came to life. Curtis continued up the stairs, the floor numbers posted on the wooden doors marking his ascent as he passed them.

He had just passed the second floor and had become accustomed to the lights buzzing on and off when another light a little higher above him suddenly clicked on.

Curtis paused mid-step, peering up past the railings to see who else had come into the stairwell. He hadn't thought many of the other residents cared to use these stairs. Then again, if the elevator wasn't working in the basement, chances are it was also out for the rest of the building. Still, the main stairwell was a much better option. Well-lit, softly carpeted, nothing at all like this barren, grey hellscape.

The light above clicked off again and no others turned on to mark the passage of whoever was up there.

Trying not to think about it too hard, Curtis started up the stairs again. As he reached the third floor, and the light behind him clicked off, another light, much closer this time, flicked on.

The light above Curtis did not.

He stopped again, shrouded in shadow, and peered toward the light. He just caught the tail-end of someone as they disappeared around the corner of the stairwell, but not enough to make out any detail or to identify which of his neighbours it was. The light above him suddenly flared to life as the one ahead darkened. His veins were filled with ice, and he began to move faster, the promise of his apartment so close, yet frustratingly far. As he turned the corner, Curtis again caught the shape of someone rounding the next bend ahead, and this time he could make out more detail. A small frame. Pale skin, almost grey under the harsh fluorescent light. Long flowing hair, as dark as night.

His breath caught, and Curtis found himself slowing down.

As he reached the next corner, he could see that the next set of lights hadn't yet timed out. He turned the corner, heart beating out of his chest, not knowing who or what would be waiting for him there. But the stairwell was empty.

When he finally reached the door marking the fourth floor, Curtis wanted to cry with relief. He spilled out through the heavy wooden door and paced down the hallway as quickly as he could toward his apartment. Rounding the final corner, Curtis's steps slowed. His apartment door was wide open.

Had he left it that way? He didn't think he had, but his mind hadn't exactly been on a straight track the last couple of days. The closer he got to the warm and welcoming lights spilling from his entranceway, the looser his body felt, the tension melting away as his sanctuary neared.

Then the door slammed shut.

Chapter Four

A panicked cry escaped him, and he raced the last few steps to the door.

The knob turned easily under his hand, and cautiously, he peered around it and into his living space.

There were no sounds and there was no movement. The place was empty.

A breeze from the stairwell? he thought to himself as he stepped through the door, closing and locking it behind him.

The rational part of Curtis's mind knew that wasn't the case, but then the rational part of his mind also knew that he'd thrown the same damn box out three times already, and yet each time it had found its way back inside his apartment. Thinking of the box as though it was some kind of sentient creature made Curtis's stomach tighten and churn.

He carried his fresh laundry into his room, setting the basket down while surveying the area. He checked the rest of the apartment, but the box wasn't there.

Feeling victorious—although why, he didn't know—Curtis had set about making dinner for himself. He ate at his dining nook while scrolling through Facebook.

His feed was full of the usual crap until suddenly Lilah's face was smiling out at him from the screen. Curtis dropped his fork in surprise, the silverware clattering off his plate.

It was a picture of Lilah and Emily, one of her friends from Oak River, and based on the familiar background of Lisandro's Italian restaurant, she was in town.

Curtis felt his heart swell as he thought about the possibilities.

Would she seek him out? How long was she sticking around for? He needed to see her!

Emily had very helpfully tagged Lilah in the picture. Lilah had always hated social media and refused to join, but travelling the country probably pushed her into creating an account so she could easily keep in touch with her girlfriends and her family.

He hit the "Add Friend" button, then dropped his phone on the table and pushed it away, as though Lilah could see him through the screen. He released an unsteady breath and grinned.

Lilah was back in town!

Grabbing a Budweiser from the fridge, he padded out to the living room and dropped onto the couch.

An hour later, his phone buzzed, and he raced to the kitchen to grab it. Lilah had accepted his friend request. He double-checked his alarm for work in the morning, then turned the phone off. He needed to get his head on straight if he was going to have a shot with Lilah. Sleep was the best thing for him.

Heading into his bedroom, Curtis noticed the bathroom door was ajar, a rectangle of light slicing into the darkened hallway and framing the wall opposite. He opened it wider to flick off the light and froze.

The box sat upon the textured grey rug by the shower. One flap was raised, and what looked like the crown of a dark head was barely visible above the rim of the box. A shuddering wheeze filled the air around the box. The head began to rise.

Curtis screamed and ran toward the closest room to him. Slamming his bedroom door behind him, he clicked the lock, and then for good measure, he grabbed the chair from the small desk and jammed it under the knob.

Dropping to the floor, Curtis watched beneath the crack in the door.

Something was approaching.

He could see the shadows twist and move as it drew closer. His eyes widened as two bare feet came to a stop outside.

Lifting himself up onto his elbows, Curtis blinked rapidly, his mind trying to comprehend what he was seeing. He dropped back to the floor.

The feet were gone, but in their stead was one half of a face, a single visible eye, as black as an abyss, gazing at him from beneath the door. The thing's half-mouth curled into a sneer, a long, rasping breath escaping from between lips that were so drained of colour they were practically grey.

Scrabbling back from the door, Curtis dived into his bed. The mattress was bare, as were the pillows, since his overwrought mind hadn't thought to replace the covers.

With a whimper, he looked on as the shadows beneath the door alternated. The rasping and wheezing continued, and Curtis realised that it was calling to him.

"Curtisssss."

"How the fuck does it know my name?!" he whispered to himself.

With growing horror, Curtis watched as the shadows within the strip of light coalesced, and long alabaster fingers began creeping beneath the crack under the door. They skittered along the carpet, both sets of fingers crossing the threshold onto his side of the barrier. It was horrific to behold.

Curtis screamed again with every ounce of strength he had, hoping someone in the building would hear him and . . . do what? He had no idea what he was dealing with and no idea if anyone could help him. His throat raw, Curtis lay down, pulling the pillow over his head and the blanket over it. He had lain there, tears glistening on his cheeks, crying softly to himself, even after the thing beyond the door had stopped calling his name. He had heard it pad softly back down the hall to the bathroom, then the soft rustle of cardboard that preceded the silence. And even then, he had continued to cry.

And now it was morning. Monday morning, no less, and he had work to attend. Still, work was better than being in his apartment with that *thing*. He looked like shit and felt like it, too, because he had barely slept, if at all. The bathroom door had been closed this morning, and he had been too afraid to venture in.

Tim would be here any minute to pick him up.

As if on cue, his phone buzzed with a message from his friend, letting Curtis know that he was in the parking lot. With a heavy sigh, Curtis pocketed his phone and keys and left the apartment. He had a plan, he just hoped it would work.

Tim stared at Curtis in disbelief.

Curtis couldn't blame him, but he felt lighter somehow, having shared the horrifying weekend he had endured with his friend and colleague. He had known his rougher-than-usual appearance wouldn't go unnoticed, but he hadn't expected to see the level of concern that was written all over Tim's face as he had hauled himself into the truck.

A gentle push from Tim had been all that was needed for him to spill his guts, tears pricking his eyes the entire time, threatening to spill over. He didn't know if Tim believed his story, but he was clearly concerned for Curtis regardless of whether the strange goings-on were real or imaginary. He instantly suggested that Curtis go back to his apartment, pack a bag, and come stay with him and his family for a few days. Curtis eschewed that idea right off the bat. No way was he bringing his problems to his friend's doorstep, especially with Bella to think of.

She was only four years old and the absolute light of her parents' lives. She was a clever little girl who shunned princesses and glitter for space rockets and hunting down bugs in the garden. She never failed to make Curtis smile anytime he visited their home. Bella was an unofficial niece in his eyes, and there was no way in hell he was risking anything bad happening to her. He knew Tim wouldn't risk it either, and that in itself told him that he most likely thought Curtis was delusional. But Tim was a good friend, so he didn't say as much out loud, and he was willing to help in any way he could to ease the burden on Curtis's shoulders.

"So, lunchtime," Tim said, looking earnestly to Curtis, "we'll head over to that weird chick's house to see what she knows about this box and, more importantly, to get her to take the fuckin' thing back!"

Curtis nodded in agreement.

"If she doesn't want to talk or refuses to take it back, then the plan is to just take it there anyway this evening."

Tim grunted his concurrence, and with a roar, the truck's engine came to life. They rolled out of the parking lot and headed to work.

The hours until lunchtime crept along slowly, and Curtis struggled to keep his mind on the job.

More than once, he had almost stepped in front of a car, each time the loud honking and angry yells dragging him back to the present. He caught Tim looking at him with concern on more than one occasion. But finally, one o'clock rolled around.

Tim let the truck crawl along the leafy suburban street until Curtis leaned across him and pointed at one of the well-kept clapboard houses.

"That's it! That's the one," he said, his finger directing Tim's eyes to a house with a blue and white painted mailbox at the end of a short walkway bordered by colourful flowers.

A FOR SALE sign stood erect on the manicured lawn. Plastered across it was a woman's face beaming with a thousand-watt smile and perfectly coiffed brown hair.

"You have got to be shitting me!" Curtis said.

Before the truck had come to a stop, he was out the passenger side door and hurrying up the walkway, the fragrant scent of flowers engulfing him as he passed. He ran up the wooden steps and knocked on the door with urgency. No answer.

He hammered his fist on the door, calling out to whoever was inside.

"Hey, lady! I need to talk to you real bad about that box."

But nobody came to the door, and the longer Curtis stood there, he realised he couldn't hear any of the usual sounds that droned from every other house.

No kids shouting and laughing. No radio or TV blaring. No footsteps.

With a curse of annoyance and desperation, Curtis made his way back to the truck, scanning the surrounding area as he went. The door of the adjacent house opened suddenly, and a harried-looking woman with a crying baby on her hip stepped outside and headed for her mailbox.

"Hey, excuse me," said Curtis. "Do you know where the lady that lives here is, by any chance? I need to find her; I have something that belongs to her, and I need to return it."

The woman stopped, bouncing the baby on her hip as she surveyed him.

"Cathy's her name," she finally said, lifting her free hand to shield her eyes from the afternoon sun. "Didn't know her well, but she always seemed nice enough. Hasn't looked herself the past few weeks. Saw her haul ass out of there Saturday morning, the realtor's sign went up later that day, and I haven't seen her since. Figured maybe a bad ex-boyfriend or something was hassling her, so she needed to disappear fast. It'd explain why she's looked so jittery lately. I shouted hello to her last week when she was at the mailbox, and I shit you not, she screamed!"

The woman chuckled a little at that, no doubt recalling the incident with her neighbour.

"Did she happen to leave a forwarding address with you? Or is there anyone on the street she might have left one with?" asked Curtis hopefully.

"Doubt it," said the woman. "Check with her, maybe." She nodded toward the FOR SALE sign jutting out of the grass.

"Of course!" exclaimed Curtis, slapping a hand to his face. "Thank you so much!"

The woman grunted and waved a hand in response, grabbing her mail and heading back inside the house.

As Curtis pulled himself into the cab of the truck, Tim looked at him expectantly.

"So, are we heading to the realtor's office now or after work?"

"I'll give them a call while we eat. I'm not cutting into any more of your downtime," Curtis replied. Tim put his foot on the gas, and they lurched forward.

After another few minutes of navigating the suburban streets, they pulled into the McDonald's Drive Thru. While Tim ordered burgers and fries, Curtis opened Google on his cell phone and searched for the realtor's number. He dialled and listened to it ring only once before the call was answered by a friendly female voice.

It turned out to be Miss I'm-on-a-sign herself, and despite being very friendly, she was no help. She told him that she did, in fact, have a forwarding address for the client he was looking for, but the woman had specifically requested that it not be passed out to anybody. She told him she'd be more than happy to take a message for Cathy and relay it to her on his behalf.

Curtis gritted his teeth. There was no way he could recount his story to this stranger, and he definitely didn't think she'd pass it along to Cathy.

"Just tell her that Curtis, the garbage man, called. She gave me something a few days ago and I really need her to take it back urgently."

The woman took his contact details and assured him she would pass them to Cathy, along with his message. Hanging up the phone, he sighed wearily. Tim glanced over, shoving a bag across the truck onto his lap.

"You've done what you can, dude. Eat up and try to relax. We'll sort this whole mess out one way or another."

Curtis gave his friend a grateful smile, then tore into the food. The longer he was out of the apartment, the more he relaxed, and the more he relaxed, the hungrier he felt.

Maybe I could market the box as some kind of ultimate diet, he smirked to himself.

His mind flashed to the creeping fingers beneath his bedroom door last night and he quickly sobered.

Chapter Five

As the day carried on and finishing time drew ever closer, Curtis could feel himself becoming more and more tense.

Tim noticed it, too, because as they left work together, he offered to drive them both to Broderick's instead. Tim rarely went to Broderick's beyond a Friday night, preferring to spend the rest of his free time at home with his wife and daughter. For him to offer up his Monday evening showed Curtis just how concerned his friend was for him.

He waved away the idea, swallowing down the apprehension he felt at the thought of going home. He needed to face that thing from the box. It was his apartment, and he shouldn't need to avoid it. These thoughts rattled around inside his head as he said his goodbyes to Tim and headed into his building. Inside the elevator, the lights flickered but Curtis chose to ignore them. As he walked through his door, he noticed the box was back in the kitchen, but he chose to ignore it too.

Proud of himself for staying strong, Curtis headed for the shower. As the steaming water cascaded down his body, he heard the bathroom door hit the tiled wall behind it as it flew open. His body somehow managed to break out in gooseflesh despite the warmth of the water, and through the distorted glass, he watched a shadowy figure enter the room. His stomach sank.

In a flash, the figure had moved and was across the room, its pale hands splayed upon the steamed glass of the shower. Its dark eyes locked on to Curtis's, and it smiled at him, a horrifying grin that seemed too wide for its grotesquely small and feminine face.

Curtis shouted in fear and jolted back as the thing smacked its palms against the partition. The sudden movement made him slip on the slick floor, and Curtis went down heavily, his head knocking off the hard tiles of the shower. He lay sprawled in the shower tray, dazed, watching a thin ribbon of crimson twist through the clear water before everything went black.

With a wince, Curtis rubbed the tender knot on the back of his head, a painful reminder of the previous evening.

After coming to in the shower—the water now almost freezing as it needled his broken body—he had limped dejectedly to his bedroom to dry and dress. After tending to his bangs and scrapes, Curtis settled down to watch TV with another takeout meal.

He had spent the evening jumpy and afraid and feeling more than a little sorry for himself. Needing a connection, something to remind him that things weren't all bad, Curtis had reached out to Lilah through Facebook.

Within a couple of texts, they had settled back into the familiarity of each other. For the first time in days, his heart had felt light, and he had genuinely smiled. They had agreed to meet on Wednesday night at Broderick's for a drink or two and to catch up in person.

The prospect of seeing Lilah in the flesh after such a long absence excited him, and feeling more positive than he had in days, he went to bed. He didn't know if it was the power of positivity or some other reason, but the ghoulish woman from the box left him alone for the rest of the night.

He had woken briefly during the night, aware of a noise from the hallway outside his bedroom door. Terrified that she was about to begin her haunting, he had stiffened in the bed as he strained his ears to listen. He could hear the soft movement of her feet across the carpeted hallway, but she didn't stop by his door. It was as though she were on parade, moving up the length of the hallway and then returning again, over and over. Eventually, the soft susurration of her bare feet on the carpet lulled him back to sleep. It was the best sleep Curtis had had since Friday.

It was lunchtime now and he decided it was time to check in with the realtor. Sure, it had only been a day, but he had let her know that the message was urgent. The phone rang in his ear, and once again, she answered in a cheery tone. After Curtis had identified himself, her tone changed.

Her client, she had informed him, wanted no further messages relayed to her from Curtis. She did not know him, he had nothing that belonged to her, and she didn't appreciate strangers contacting her. Curtis tried to protest, but the realtor shut him down, said she also wanted to hear nothing further from him, and then hung up.

Curtis looked at his phone in disbelief, the quiet beeping from the disconnected call still audible.

Tim looked over at his friend, reading his expression in an instant.

"Screw them bitches," he said, trying to lighten the desperation emanating from Curtis like a heavy fog rolling off the sea.

Curtis put his head in his hands and exhaled heavily.

"I have no idea what to do. I can't keep living like this, and no matter what I do with the box, it just shows up again!"

Tim said nothing, for there was nothing to be said. He had offered to come up to the apartment and take the box, but Curtis was unwilling to risk dragging anyone else into whatever the hell was going on with him. It killed Tim to watch from the sidelines as his best friend unravelled, but other than just being there for Curt when he needed to talk, there was little else he could do.

"Your Angie is really into all the weird paranormal stuff, right?" Curtis asked, turning to Tim with suddenly hopeful eyes.

Tim nodded cautiously in response.

"I know I asked you not to say anything about what's been going on, but maybe it's time to tell Angie and see if she knows someone who might be able to help. I know nothing about this stuff. Shit, I never expected to ever be dealing with something like this!"

Curtis was desperate, and he knew that by allowing Tim to share this with his wife, his best friend would understand just how desperate he was.

"Sure, I can ask her," he replied slowly, "she knows a ton of spiritual people. I'm pretty sure she's even been to stores that sell all the hoodoo-voodoo crap. Tell you what, how about you head over to the deli and grab lunch for us before time's up, and I'll call her right now to see if she has any good ideas."

Curtis nearly crumpled with relief, then instantly thought of the woman, Cathy, who had reacted similarly when he had taken the box from her.

Anger swelled inside him, sharp and hot, as he thought about how she had selfishly and knowingly passed that box to him.

Shaking his head to dislodge the thoughts, he aimed a grateful smile at Tim and slid from the truck. There was no point dwelling on the actions of that woman. The box was in his possession now, and unless Angie could help, there was nothing he could do about it.

"Maybe I could give her a name and we could live like the people in those odd couple shows on TV," he said to himself with a chuckle.

It was easy to think like that after one relatively quiet night, but every time his mind flashed back to those ghastly fingers beneath his bedroom door or the pale, flat palms slapping against the glass of the shower, he knew he hadn't seen the worst of what was to come.

Curtis reached the deli, pausing briefly to scan the poster on the door announcing the upcoming Spring Fling festival. The poster was garish, and the array of colours almost hurt his eyes, but he smiled nonetheless. He vaguely remembered Bella excitedly chattering about a competition being held for all the local kids to design posters and flyers for the festival. As he pushed the door open, he wondered idly if Bella had entered. He'd have to ask Tim about it.

As he stepped through the heavy door to the establishment, a small bell tinkled above it, announcing his entry.

"Curt!"

He turned toward the voice. He would have known that gentle cadence anywhere.

"Lilah!" he said, smiling warmly and stepping forward to envelop her in his arms. She leaned into him heavily, the soft scent of her jasmine shampoo filling his senses.

"The usual, Curtis?" called Maria, the proprietor, from behind the counter.

Lilah stepped back from his embrace, a shy smile on her face.

Curtis shot a grin and a thumbs up toward Maria, and with a knowing smile and a shake of her head, she busied herself behind the counter, preparing the food.

"So, have you told anyone about our date tomorrow?" he asked Lilah, leaning around her to wave at her friend Emily, who grinned and wiggled her fingers at him in return.

"Oh, it's a date now?" She smiled up at him, the light through the plate glass window catching her hair and turning it golden.

"It's absolutely a date, and we all knew about it before you two had even arranged it!" Emily called sweetly.

"Even I knew." Maria laughed.

Lilah looked down shyly, her cheeks tinting the subtlest shade of pink. Curtis could feel his heart squeeze. God, he loved that girl so much.

They talked easily until Maria called Curtis to collect his order. Saying his goodbyes, he paid Maria and scooped the paper bag off the counter, the bell jingling this time to announce his departure. He could feel Lilah's eyes on him as he strolled past the window and away from the deli. Feeling like his face might split from grinning so hard, Curtis pulled open the truck door and jumped in.

"Well shit, aren't you in a better mood! Food really does fix everything," Tim said in amusement.

"Lilah was in the deli with Emily," replied Curtis, unable to wipe the smile from his face.

Tim chuckled.

"If your date tomorrow goes well, she might decide against skipping town again. Maybe you could make a proper go of things. Marriage, babies, it's all ahead of you, brother! And don't worry about coming in for work tomorrow. Take the day to do what you need to." He winked.

Curtis threw his head back and laughed. He hadn't felt this good in days, and he willed the feeling to stay with him for as long as he could hold onto it.

"Angie was enthralled by your . . . strange occurrences. Wanted me to ask you if she and some of her spiritual friends could set up a séance in your apartment. I told her you didn't need to summon anything, it's rid of the damn thing you need!"

Curtis snorted.

"So anyway," continued Tim, "she says that little old guy in the curio shop on Main could be exactly who you need. Says he's well known among the 'spiritual types' for being able to break hexes and all kinds of weird shit. Can you believe it? A fuckin' exorcist setting up shop right there on Main! Jeff and the other sycophantic bastards in the mayor's office mustn't know. There's no way they'd have dirty demon dollars sullying their tax fund!"

With that, the two men doubled over laughing, their sides aching and their eyes streaming.

"At least now I know I have options," Curtis finally said, as his laughter subsided.

It felt good to laugh.

"You sure you don't want to drop in there and have a chat with him?" asked Tim.

"Nah," replied Curtis. "If things don't improve, though, I'll definitely stop by."

They ate in companionable silence, the peace only broken by the occasional rustle of wrappers and slurping of cold drinks. When their lunch hour was up, they took off back to work. The hours passed quickly, and when finishing time rolled around, Curtis could feel the now familiar tension descending upon him. But it wasn't as bad as it had been, and for that, he was grateful.

Chapter Six

Running a polished nail over the rim of her glass absentmindedly, Lilah threw her head back in laughter, her long, glossy hair tumbling down her back. Curtis grinned at her over the rim of his own glass. Their date was going well so far. They had slotted back into each other's company so easily, as though they had both been missing some vital piece that was now within reach. The evening so far had been filled with flirtatious banter, and Curtis was pretty sure he knew where things were headed. He didn't think either of them would be leaving Broderick's alone.

He reclined in his chair, grimacing slightly as his back hit the seat. The previous night had been much like the one before. The thing from the box had given him a wide berth, then commenced pacing in the hall after he had gone to bed. But in letting his guard down, Curtis had forgotten to lock his bedroom door, and when he had awoken that morning, he was greeted with fresh pain. A cursory examination in the mirror showed long grooves gouged down his back. The scratches weren't deep, but they stung. Even now, too much pressure in their general vicinity left him flinching. He pulled his mind back to the beautiful girl before him.

"Are you still driving that piece of crap Chevy?" he teased.

Lilah smirked at him and opened her mouth to reply, then stopped and leaned across toward him. She reached out and plucked something from his shirt. The smile faltered on her face as she held the long dark hair aloft.

"Someone you need to tell me about?"

Lilah tried to sound casual, but Curtis could detect the note of hurt in her voice.

Shit.

"No, nobody. I have no idea where that came from. Probably brushed against someone at the bar," he replied cautiously.

He cursed himself inwardly for not being prepared for something like this. Panic blossomed in the pit of his stomach at the thought of Lilah coming home to his apartment. He knew that was where the night was headed. She knew it too. They were too in sync with one another, and both of them had felt the electric atmosphere that had crackled between them all night.

Screw it, Curtis thought to himself. If Lilah came back and saw the woman for herself, at least he'd know for sure he wasn't crazy because, at this point, he was beginning to question his own sanity.

As time passed and the bar slowly emptied around them, Curtis and Lilah continued to talk, heads close together, arms touching.

"I think it's time we leave," said Lilah, nodding her head toward Jim, the barman who had been rubbing the same spot with a towel for longer than necessary.

Curtis winced and threw Jim an apologetic wave.

"Shit, sorry, Jimbo!" he said. "We'll get out of your hair now."

Jim nodded and chuckled before turning back to stack freshly cleaned glasses.

Lilah held his arm as they strolled out onto the dark street, giggling like a schoolgirl as though his wit was the finest she had ever encountered.

They hailed a cab, Curtis holding the door open for her in a chivalrous gesture. She smiled at him, her eyes probing his as she slid into the car ahead of him.

"Where to?" asked the grizzled old man up front.

They looked at each other. Curtis could feel his pulse quicken as he looked into Lilah's eyes. He could see the desire he felt reflected in her own blue eyes. She smiled at him, a devilish grin, then she turned her head and reeled off his address to the driver. Without another word, she lay back against him, the smell of her perfume intoxicating his senses.

As the car pulled up in front of his building, Curtis pulled a wad of notes from his pocket.

"Keep the change!" he called to the driver as Lilah pulled him by the hand from the vehicle.

They stumbled into the lobby, the sounds of their giggling and theatrical whispering echoing around the empty foyer. The elevator stood waiting to receive them, the doors sliding open as soon as the button was pressed. They fell through the opening and into each other's arms before the doors had time to slide shut again.

By the time the elevator dinged to announce their arrival on the fourth floor, Curtis was practically panting. His hair was tousled from Lilah's exploratory hands.

He had missed her so much.

They crashed through the apartment door, wrapped in each other. Clothes were peeled off and tossed in every direction as they pushed and pulled their way to Curtis's bedroom, a tango that was so familiar to them both despite the passing of time.

Curtis worshipped Lilah. She was a goddess, and he happily bowed before her, bringing her to dizzying heights of pleasure.

When they were both sated, they dropped panting, sweat glistening on both of their bodies as the heavy slumber of the deeply satisfied took them both. Curtis hadn't felt this happy in a long time. The dark-haired woman even seemed to stay put that night, never moving from her box to stalk the hallways. Pulling Lilah's gently snoring frame closer to him, Curtis thanked the universe, or whatever it was that had sent Lilah back into his life. He wouldn't mess things up this time.

Dull light crept through the window, pulling Curtis from his slumber.

Their bodies had separated through the night, but through squinted eyes he could just make out Lilah's small form on the other side of the bed. In the murky gloom, she was nothing more than a pile of shadows. Closing his eyes again and allowing slumber to pull him back down heavily, he turned toward her, reaching an arm out to rest on her side. She was no longer beneath the blanket and her skin felt cool. Curtis was more than happy to fix that problem. He tugged her body toward him, pulling her close to his chest. With a breathy sigh, she nuzzled in closer. Her hair spilled across his bare skin and Curtis opened his eyes and glanced down, his heart warmed by her presence.

The strands that fanned out from her head were as black as night.

Curtis jolted back, his eyes widening as he looked at the form beside him. The ghoul stared back at him with an impenetrable gaze and a hideous grin that almost split its ghostly face in two.

"Curtisss."

Its voice was like nails on a chalkboard to his ears, the guttural hiss turning to throaty laughter.

With a shriek, Curtis tumbled out of bed, knocking the bedside locker over as he fell and landed heavily on his back. The wind was knocked from his lungs, and he lay there on the floor, scrabbling for air as the wretched woman pulled herself across the bed.

Her withered hands grasped the edge of the bed, and she slid down beside him, crawling along the floor, pulling herself closer and closer.

Curtis watched in frozen horror as she manoeuvred herself, crawling up onto his chest until their faces were practically touching. Her eyes seemed to hold everything and nothing all at once, as dead as ashes but somehow still full of the fire that had created them.

"Curtissss."

She leaned closer, so close that he could feel, as well as hear, the wet rasping of her rattling chest. An overwhelming smell of death and decay enveloped his senses, and he could feel his stomach roil in response. She whispered in his ear, murmuring in hushed tones and foreign tongue. Curtis could feel himself slipping away from reality as he lay immobile on his bedroom floor. The last thing he remembered was the oddly hypnotic way the dust motes danced and twirled in the pale light of a breaking dawn.

Curtis woke in bed, the blanket pooling around his waist. He stretched and yawned, and the memories of what had happened suddenly came crashing in around him.

It had to have been a nightmare.

He looked over at the empty half of the big bed, his eyes immediately falling on the black strands that lay on the pillow resting beside his own. He snapped his head around to where the locker still lay on its side, the contents spilled haphazardly around it.

"Fuck!" he said aloud.

He ran shaking hands through his chestnut hair, his eyes wide and wild. More memories flooded in.

The woman's face just inches from his own as she whispered her horrible ruminations in his ear. Her hands clawed at the edge of the bed as she twisted her way closer to him. Lilah's golden head tucked neatly into the crook of his arm, a satisfied smile on her face. He and Lilah's bodies writhing as one. The scent of her perfume as they melded together in the elevator. The woman. Lilah. The woman.

Lilah!

He sprang from the bed, forgetting the fear and the tension in his body.

Where did Lilah go?

Had she seen the woman?

She would have woken him if that was the case. Wouldn't she?

He raced to the kitchen, but nothing was out of place. Until a scrap of paper stuck to the refrigerator caught his eye. He snatched it from the gleaming surface.

Goodbye, Curt.

That was it.

Two words in Lilah's looping cursive. He ran back to his bedroom, rooting in the trail of fallen clothing until he found his phone. He grasped it in both hands and dialled her number.

Two rings and the call disconnected.

He typed a frantic message and hit send, watching as the symbol changed to notify him that it had been read. He watched as the little dots appeared, holding his breath as the dots continued to dance on the small screen.

Walking back into the kitchen to put on a pot of coffee, he felt the phone vibrate in his hand. It was Lilah telling him to leave her alone.

In confusion, Curtis dialled her number again.

"What do you want, Curt?" she said, picking up almost instantly.

"Lilah, are you okay? What's going on? Why did you leave without saying anything?" he asked.

"Am I okay?" she snorted, "Of course I'm not okay, Curt. You lied to me. You let me believe that we had a proper chance this time, and it was all so you could get me back to your place to be another notch on your bedpost. Well, I don't think it counts as another notch if we have history."

"Lilah, I have no idea what you're talking about. We do have a proper chance. I love you, and I don't know what's happened since last night but, Jesus, just talk to me. Tell me what I need to do to make this right."

"The hair I picked off you at the bar," she said quietly, hurt evident in her voice, "I spent half the night pulling them from your bed. Not to mention the scratches on your back! You couldn't even be bothered to change your sheets afterwards?? I don't care who she is, and I don't care if it's serious or not. You should have *told* me, Curt."

Her voice broke, and Curtis's stomach dropped.

"Lilah, I . . ."

"No, Curt, I can't listen to excuses. I even took a sweater from your cupboard before I left because I had no jacket, and guess what I found on it? That's right. Another fucking hair, Curtis. She left enough hair around your place that I wouldn't be surprised if she's bald now! I put it back, so don't worry about waiting for it to be returned," she said bitterly.

"Lilah, can you please let me explain?" he said desperately, "It's going to sound crazy, but I think I'm cursed, or being haunted at the very least. Those hairs don't belong to any woman I've been involved with."

"Fuck, Curtis, don't give me that bullshit. Fuck! Even now, with things on the line, you're still the same old Curt. Any excuse is better than the truth. I'm leaving town today, and I don't want to hear from you again. Goodbye, Curtis."

The call disconnected.

Curtis gaped in stunned silence at the phone in his hand and exhaled a trembling breath. He dialled her number again, but this time it went straight to voicemail.

He paced the floor, running his free hand through his hair as he spoke to her mailbox, desperately trying to explain the situation in a way that might not make him sound crazy. He was failing miserably at it.

He should have told her before she came back to the apartment. But what are the chances that she would have believed him? It seemed like no matter what he did in this situation, it wouldn't have ended well. He didn't tell her, and she thought he was a piece of shit bed-hopper. If he had told her, she'd have thought he was crazy. Both scenarios ended the same way: Curtis without Lilah in his life.

Angry tears pricked his eyes. He had had enough of that box and the pasty bitch that came from within its cursed depths. He didn't know what she wanted from him, but it seemed as though, aside from terrorising him in his home, she was intent on leeching all the external joy from his life as well.

Curtis grabbed a can of lighter fluid from beneath the sink and pulled a box of matches from the kitchen drawer. He stomped down the hall and kicked the bathroom door open. The box sat there unmoving. He squirted fluid all over it, cursing it as he did. The flaps began to move, and those long, slender fingers appeared, curling around the edges.

With a shout of defiance, and before she could emerge any further, Curtis struck one of the matches and tossed it at the box. The cardboard caught alight instantly, small blue flames licking along its surface, following the trail of flammable liquid.

An unholy scream resounded from the flaming carton like a chorus of demonic voices, every one of them off-kilter. The smell of burning hair and flesh flooded the small room. Covering his nose and mouth with his hands, Curtis stalked from the room, wrenching the key from inside the door as he passed it, pulled it shut behind him, and locked it from the outside. Quickly and calmly, he dressed himself, grabbed his keys, his phone, and his wallet, and left the apartment. Tendrils of grey smoke reached out to him from beneath the bathroom door.

"Fuck you," he said with a quiet snarl, slamming the front door shut behind him.

Chapter Seven

Curtis wandered aimlessly away from his building. His feet had automatically begun to take him toward town, but he couldn't deal with people right now. His head was a whirl of emotion, his thoughts flying around with wild abandon.

He followed the quiet streets in a wide arc, heading toward the river. Solitude was the only friend he needed right now.

As he walked, his ears strained for the sounds of sirens. It was reckless of him to set the box on fire and leave, but what choice did he have? He knew he couldn't continue on like this.

As he neared the scenic lookout point by the old pedestrian bridge that spanned the Oak River, he slowed his pace and tried to empty his mind.

Curtis knew from previous incidents in his building that the original builders had taken fire safety very seriously. The newer building managers did, too, because there were regular checks. And only a couple of years ago, after a small electrical fire in one of the second-floor apartments, the entire building was kitted out with brand-new sprinkler systems in every room of every apartment. Except for the bathrooms, because who starts a fire in their bathroom? Curtis was one of the few residents who owned their apartment, so the fire safety upgrades were always heavily discounted but optional. He had paid to have the sprinkler system installed in just the kitchen, living room, and main bedroom, so a lot of damage could happen before the system kicked in. If his apartment burned down, well, that was a price he was willing to pay to remove that monster from his life.

He dropped wearily onto an old iron bench that stood close to the cliff edge overlooking the thrashing current below. The turbulent waters were mesmerising to watch.

Just as well there's a guardrail, Curtis thought to himself. *Probably saved a shit load of people from tumbling over the edge in a hypnotic trance.*

He rested for a while, eyes closed and ears listening to the delicate birdsong in the trees that surrounded him. The warm spring sun shone down on him, slowly easing the tension from his body.

His phone buzzed in his pocket, jerking Curtis awake.

He hadn't even realised he had fallen asleep, but it was hardly surprising. He had a horrible morning, and his body was aching and tired from the events of the day, coupled with the long walk out to the river. As he slid the phone from his jeans, he was surprised to see how late it had gotten. Lunchtime was long past, and the realisation caused his stomach to growl angrily.

He had a text from Tim, letting him know his friend knew things with Lilah hadn't gone well.

"Bad news travels fast," he said aloud, startling a small bird that had landed on the guardrail before him.

He dialled Tim's number. It was almost finishing time at work, and he didn't feel like walking the whole way back to his apartment. In fact, he didn't feel like going back to his apartment at all that night.

The call was short. Tim eagerly offered to pick him up from the lookout point as soon as he was done with work. He seemed relieved when Curtis suggested staying with him and Angie that night, saying he'd call Angie to let her know they had an extra head at the dinner table tonight. Bella was going to be delighted, Tim had told Curtis. She loved having Uncle Curt over to visit!

Satisfied that he had finally made a good decision that was within his control, Curtis slid the phone back into his pocket and stared at the sparkling water some more.

He didn't look away from the river until the sound of tires on gravel broke through the silence surrounding him on the iron bench. Tim's truck came to a slow halt, his friend hanging from the open window, grinning at him.

"Let's go, amigo!" he shouted, "Gotta get home and fire up the barbecue. Burger and beers sound good to you?"

"Sounds perfect."

Curtis lifted himself from the bench and made his way around the truck. His heart was still hurting over Lilah, but a seed of hope was sprouting in his stomach.

The box was gone, burnt to ashes on his bathroom floor. With that problem solved, he would do whatever it took to show Lilah he wasn't the same man she had driven away from before. The feeling that thrummed through his veins felt foreign, but only because it seemed like it had been a lifetime since he last felt it. *It* was optimism.

A cool breeze rustled through the gnarled branches of the tall trees that surrounded Tim's backyard. They stood like giant sentinels in the growing evening shadows. The sun had almost set, and the sky was aflame in hues of orange and red.

Curtis and Tim sat companionably in rocking chairs on the porch, each with a cold bottle of beer in hand. Dinner had been great, and Curtis loved seeing Bella.

She was growing like a weed, and he had silently promised himself to start coming over more often to spend time with the whole family. Tim was like a brother to him, and his family was Curtis's family too.

He could tell Angie was itching for details about what happened to sour things with Lilah so suddenly. Tim had probably warned her off asking any probing questions because he had gotten away with giving them a very diluted version of events.

He also decided it was best not to mention setting fire to his bathroom.

He knew Tim was already worried for his mental state and letting him think he had become an arsonist was unlikely to help the situation.

After dinner, he had run around the lawn with Bella. She shrieked with delight every time he caught her and tossed her into the air, her auburn curls bouncing wildly. He tagged along on one of her bug hunting adventures and helped the little girl add more insects to her terrarium.

Angie hated having the thing in the house but was quietly proud of her daughter for chasing different dreams than the other kids they knew. She had retired to the living room with a book after Bella had gone to bed. Bella had insisted on Curtis being part of the process, so he happily sat reading stories until her eyes became heavy. He tucked her in tightly, kissed her on the forehead, and bade her good night.

Tim was waiting for him in the hallway, a bottle of beer tilted in his direction. They had sat out on the porch, enjoying the fresh air after the heat of the day. Without going into too much detail, Curtis told Tim a little more about the situation with Lilah. He told his friend he planned on going after her, proving he was really serious about her this time. Hopefully, she would see that he was genuine, and it would be enough for her to return, even if it was only temporarily. If she wanted to hit the road again, then he would happily join her.

"Daddy."

The two men turned to see Bella standing in the open doorway in bare feet, her battered old stuffed dog clutched in hand.

"What's the matter, baby?" asked Tim, dropping to his knees before the little girl and brushing a fiery curl behind her ear.

"The lady is looking for Uncle Curt. She's in his room waiting for him," she replied sleepily, "She was calling him, and I don't think Mommy could hear her, so I went to see if she was okay."

Tim whipped his head around to look at Curtis, whose jaw had dropped.

"She's not very pretty, Uncle Curt." Bella leaned around her father to address the other man. "She's kind of scary."

Tim knew by the sudden wild look in Curtis's eyes that his next move could make or break however traumatising this situation was going to be for his daughter. He snapped his fingers at his friend to garner his attention, then waved his hand slowly in a "calm down" motion.

"Let's get you back to bed, baby girl," Tim said, lifting the little girl into his arms.

Curtis stood and followed them through the doorway. While Tim brought Bella back into her room, Curtis continued down the hallway to the guest room. As he approached the door, the acrid smell of smoke caught in his nostrils. He cautiously stepped inside, his eyes darting around the shadowed room. He flicked on the overhead light, but the room was empty.

Curtis knew he should be relieved, but what Bella had said was stuck in his brain.

She's kind of scary.

With a sinking feeling in the pit of his stomach, he headed back up the hallway where Tim was waiting outside Bella's bedroom, the soft glow of her nightlight leaking through the door.

Tim looked at him expectantly and he shrugged.

"A little girl with an overactive imagination." Tim laughed. "Another beer?"

"Yes, please, I'm gonna hit the head. Meet you back on deck." Curtis fake saluted his friend, who snorted in amusement.

"Aye aye, sailor!" Tim replied, turning away, his shoulders shaking with mirth.

Curtis headed to the bathroom, closing the door gently behind him so as not to disturb Bella. He relieved himself, then turned to the basin to wash his hands. Reflected in the mirror above the sink, two grey arms snaked over his shoulders.

The crown of a dark head was barely visible behind him as its splayed hands roamed across his chest, nails digging deeper and deeper. He flinched, whipping around, but there was no one there.

An anguished moan escaped his lips. She wasn't gone. He hadn't managed to destroy the box.

And now he was putting his best friend's family in danger by being here with this malevolent presence so firmly attached to him.

He lurched back down the hallway and out onto the porch. Tim looked up, concern immediately creasing his face.

"You okay, pal? You look like you've seen a ghost or some shit," Tim said.

The irony wasn't lost on Curtis.

"My stomach has taken a turn. I feel like shit," he said, and he genuinely did feel like shit. "Raincheck? I'll call a cab, head home, and get some rest."

Tim wouldn't hear of it and offered to drive Curtis back to his apartment. With apologies to Angie and a promise to come over again next week for a do-over, they left.

The closer the truck brought him to his home, the tighter his stomach felt. By the time Tim pulled up outside the building, Curtis was sure he was going to be sick. He said his goodbye, and with his body taut with nerves, he headed up in the elevator to the fourth floor.

The sense of foreboding as he walked down the hallway to his front door was almost enough to make him pass out there and then, or at the very least, run screaming from the building. His skin crawled and his scalp itched as cold fear washed over him.

He stepped inside and with a heaviness he had hoped to never feel again, he headed straight for the bathroom.

He could smell smoke, but when he turned the key and swung the door open, the box was gone. The bathroom was unblemished, though the scent of smoke hung in the air like the remnants of a bad dream. Curtis turned and went to his bedroom, hoping to shut the world out for one more night.

The box sat neatly at the foot of his bed.

Weary with desperation, Curtis ignored it and crawled into bed without undressing, pulling the blanket over his head. It was flimsy but still felt like a form of protection. In no time at all, he felt a gentle pressure as something lowered itself onto the bed by his feet.

Not something. *Her.*

He whimpered quietly to himself as she clawed and pulled her way up the mattress, coming to rest behind him. And there they lay for the night, like two lovers in an embrace. Her cold, spindly arms roving around him, trying to gain access to his skin, using her nails to mark any part of him she could touch. Curtis cried softly as the ghoul behind him murmured in his ear, draining him of all that he was.

"Curtisssss."

Curtis was a shadow of himself, and he knew it.

He had put on a brave face, a mask of normality, but there was no hiding the reflection that greeted him from every mirrored surface. His eyes, ringed and bruised, were sunken into skin that looked stretched and paper-thin. His brain was nothing more than a lacklustre fog, and he could see the sideways glances that Tim had thrown his way all morning. He knew his friend was concerned but unsure of whether or not to broach the subject. Curtis was acting as though nothing was wrong, hadn't mentioned the previous night, and he hoped his lack of forthrightness would be enough to discourage Tim from asking. His shattered mind wouldn't be able to rehash the horrors of the night.

As the weak light of dawn filtered into his bedroom, the woman slithered from his side and poured herself from the bed into the cardboard box on the floor. After hours spent fending off her onslaught as best he could, Curtis lay there, mouth agape and mind in a million pieces.

How could this be really happening to him?

He remained in his bed, too terrified to move until enough time had passed to ensure she was done terrorising him for now. He had quietly left the room, shutting the kitchen door behind him to minimise any noise, and there he had dressed and made strong coffee. He had spent the morning gulping down the hot, sugary liquid until he no longer felt like he needed to prop his eyelids open with matchsticks.

By the time Tim pulled up to collect him for work, Curtis had been sitting outside for almost an hour. Outside felt safe. Outside, he could force his mind to forget what was waiting for him in his apartment.

And now, as they began the slow, weekly slog down Main Street, he found himself glancing up the road and past the multitude of shops and buildings to where he knew a certain small man waited in the shadows, watching for their approach.

Sure enough, as they worked their way closer to the curiosities shop, Curtis could see the old-timer as he stepped into the sun, trash can grinding against the pavement behind him.

*I wonder, will he sense it on m*e? Curtis thought to himself before shaking the notion from his head. It was a ridiculous thought. How could anyone *sense* something like this?

As he reached the curb and put his hand out to the trash can, Curtis lifted his face, his tired eyes locking with the small man's dark, inquisitive ones.

The man's eyes narrowed before suddenly widening, and in that instant, Curtis knew that he knew. He really *could* sense it.

Curtis hauled the can to the truck and emptied it. As he turned to replace it, he nearly tripped over the short form before him.

There he stood, almost nose to nose with Curtis. Nose to chest, at the very least. He studied Curtis's face for a moment before whipping a card from within a deep sleeve and pressing it into Curtis's clammy hand.

"Come see me," he said quietly. "Sooner rather than later."

And with that, he turned on his heels and disappeared into the store, the empty trash can dragging along behind him.

Chapter Eight

Curtis looked at the small rectangle of paper in his hand. It was a thick card, almost black in colour, with only a few simple words embossed upon it in silver.

Mr Maddox

Curios ~ Cleansing ~ Giftware

Flipping the card over, he saw a strange symbol printed on the other side. With a shrug, he slid the card into his back pocket, but somehow, he felt lighter. He felt like there might finally be some answers waiting for him and, more importantly, a solution.

His mind flitted from each experience he had had at the hands of the crone in his apartment, to the expressive eyes of the enigmatic Mr Maddox.

Curtis wondered if the solution would come in the form of a curio, a cleansing, or something from the giftware section. The thought made him chuckle, and he smiled his first genuine smile of the day.

He glimpsed Tim from the corner of his eye, looking at him and smiling a genuine smile of his own. As soon as this was all over, Curtis would make it up to his friend. His behaviour had been odd and erratic for the past few days, and Tim had done his best to be a supportive friend. He had voiced concerns without overstepping any boundaries and had tried his best to help Curtis. He was a good friend.

"Did I see the exorcist slip you something?" Tim asked, as they continued hauling cans.

Pulling the small card from his pocket, Curtis waved it at his friend.

"Sure did! He gave me his card. Told me to come see him sooner rather than later. I think I'm gonna drop by during lunch if you don't mind eating solo."

Tim chuckled.

"I'd rather eat solo than go visit someone who makes a living slaying demons or witches or whatever it is he does," he said with a smirk. "I'll grab you something for after you're done, yeah?"

Curtis nodded appreciatively at his friend, grateful for him for the second time in as many minutes.

When lunchtime rolled around, they went their separate ways, Tim to the deli and Curtis to see Mr Maddox. He strolled casually along the street, enjoying the pleasant warmth of the afternoon sun. Brightly coloured festival bunting danced gently above him in the warm spring breeze and birds sang out as though announcing the upcoming festivities. Then he caught sight of his reflection in the plate glass shop fronts as he passed them and felt ice flood his veins.

The ghoul from the box was pacing along directly behind him, her dark hair curtained over most of her face. Her head was turned toward the reflection as though she knew he had become aware of her presence. One horrible eye and a half grin leered out at him from between the stringy locks.

Swallowing heavily, Curtis looked away. He had to be imagining it. How could she be out here, in broad daylight, undetected by anybody else? Plenty of people were passing him by, the spring sunshine drawing many from their homes, and nobody had screamed or pointed, or even passed comment yet.

With a heavy gulp, he turned his head back toward the glass.

There she was.

Dancing along behind him in an uneven gait, she stepped lightly on the balls of her feet like a marionette come to life. It was disturbing to watch.

Curtis stopped dead, yelping as something smacked into him from behind.

Reeling around with wide, frightened eyes, he was surprised to see a young woman looking at him with annoyance. She pulled her headphones from her ears and snarled at him.

"Watch where you're going, dude! No need to slam on the brakes so suddenly!"

And with that, she was gone, stomping off ahead of him and only looking back once to give him the finger.

Catching his breath, Curtis turned back to look at his reflection. There was nobody else around him. He was alone.

"You were behind me. Maybe *you* should have watched where *you* were going," he muttered under his breath as the girl disappeared around a corner up ahead, her blonde ponytail swinging as she turned.

As Curtis drew closer to the curiosities shop, an exotic, spicy scent seemed to waft toward him. Stopping in the shaded doorway, he peered through the gaps in the glass door.

Flyers for missing pets, babysitters, and guitar lessons covered much of its surface, and a colourful hand-drawn poster announcing the Spring Fling was taped dead centre among the rest. With a deep breath and a sigh of resignation, he pushed open the door.

Long, dangling chimes tinkled delicately as he entered. It was a pleasant sound but to his dismay, upon closer inspection, he could see the chimes were made from tiny, fragile-looking bones. In the context of everything he had been going through, it was insignificant, yet uneasiness cloaked him like a shroud.

"Good. You came."

The sudden emergence of a voice behind him as he studied the bone chime startled Curtis. He turned, offering a small smile to the man before him. Mr Maddox.

"I . . . Ummm . . . I thought maybe you could help me. I've heard you deal in some . . . unusual situations, and you clearly knew I needed some help. You gave me your card." Curtis stumbled over his words, pulling the black card from his pocket and brandishing it like a talisman.

"It's okay, calm yourself. I did indeed give you my card because I knew the moment I looked at you that there were nefarious forces at play in your life. I see you weekly and have done for years, but today, there is an aura hanging around you like a storm cloud. Such a sudden change requires swift action."

Leaning past Curtis, he flipped the sign on the door to CLOSED and flicked the latch. As the small man moved, a necklace swung into view. It was a long leather string with a delicate, silvery version of the symbol from the business card hanging from the end and catching the shafts of light that pierced the glass doorway. Mr Maddox tucked the chain back into the folds of his robe and gestured for Curtis to follow him, then turned and crossed the room. He moved so quickly and silently, it seemed as though he were floating, and Curtis became aware once more of the unease that prickled his skin.

The small man led him into a wood-panelled room in the back of the store.

The walls were lined with shelves, many of which were stuffed with books. Strange titles and Latin words were scrawled across many of the spines, and a large number of them looked older than the town of Oak River itself. Curtis gazed around the room, taking in the variety of items on display.

Glass bottles in all kinds of colours and shapes, crystals and rocks of varying sizes and textures, animal skulls and more than one human-looking skull, more books, and stacks of what looked like leatherbound journals adorned the walls. A small mahogany desk sat at the back of the room, its surface littered with an array of ink bottles, writing quills, ballpoint pens, and more writing journals.

The back wall of the room behind the desk was covered from floor to ceiling in a huge glass case, the handles of which were draped in metallic chains secured by an intricately designed padlock that held the same symbol as the card and the necklace.

The case was filled with boxes. Small stone boxes, large wooden ones, each carved with images and symbols that were completely foreign to Curtis's eyes.

Mr Maddox stood quietly for a few moments, allowing Curtis to take in his surroundings before speaking again.

"What is your name, son?" he asked.

His eyes were probing, and Curtis felt as though the man were looking right into his soul.

"I'm Curtis," he said, extending his hand politely. "Do you have a first name, or should I just call you Mr Maddox?"

"Most people just call me Mr Maddox, but you are free to call me by my name," he said, taking Curtis's outstretched hand in both of his and squeezing reassuringly. "It's Mads."

Curtis looked at him in disbelief, his lips curling into a small smile.

"Your name is Mads Maddox?" he asked, a hint of humour in his voice.

The old man chuckled and nodded gleefully.

He clearly delighted in telling folk his unusually similar names. The oddness of the whole situation was succeeding in reducing Curtis's tension, and he was glad of it.

"Mads Maddox," he said incredulously. "Mads it is!"

With a warm smile, Mads said, "Tell me, Curtis, what has been happening to you? And please start from the very beginning. Spare no detail, no matter how insignificant you may think it is."

Curtis proceeded to relay the events of the past week. His mind could hardly wrap itself around the fact that it had only been a week. How quickly our beliefs and our place in this world can be completely turned on their head.

Mads listened intently, nodding occasionally and murmuring here and there as Curtis spoke of all that had happened. As he finished speaking, his phone vibrated in his pocket. Sliding it out, he saw Tim's name on the screen and caught sight of the time.

"Shit! I need to get back to work!" he exclaimed.

"No problem, no problem at all," Mads said with a dismissive wave. "You go ahead. But come back to me after work and I should have more answers for you. I'm pretty sure I know what we are dealing with, and it will give me time to try and prepare something for you."

Hearing the man use the word "we" touched Curtis. It made him feel less alone than he had all week. Tim was his best friend, and he owed him a lot, but he couldn't be honest about the situation with him. He knew the first time he tried last weekend that Tim thought he was nuts! And who could blame him?

Curtis was almost thirty and still living alone, with no girlfriend and no interest in pursuing a career outside of garbage collection. He had no family, and the only reason he had a roof over his head was due to his grandmother's diligence. She had been the only family Curtis had and had raised him from a very young age when his parents and older sister, Bethany, were killed by a drunk driver in a head-on collision on their way home from Bethany's school play one Christmas.

Gramma Tessa had made sure Curtis wanted for nothing throughout his life, and as the cancer had prepared to finally take her, she had willed everything to him on the condition that he sold the farmhouse and bought something closer to town so he couldn't isolate himself in her absence.

A few weeks after her funeral, he had numbly signed whatever her attorney had put before him and allowed the man to follow his grandmother's wishes. The farm was sold quickly, and the attorney, Mr Peterson, had found potentially suitable real estate options for Curtis. He had bought the apartment not because he had felt any particular affinity to it, but because he was a boy who very much missed his grandmother and didn't want to deal with the intrusions of the outside world. As Mr Peterson had shown him different printouts of various properties, he had pointed at random and said, "That one."

He had grown to love his apartment, the beautiful view, its proximity to town while still maintaining the surrounding tranquillity of nature, and he had been careful with what was left of the money from his grandmother. He kept it all in a separate account so that, should he meet the girl of his dreams and settle down, he would have the funds to lay the foundation for the rest of their lives. He had hoped that girl would be Lilah. Still hoped it would be her if he could ever rid himself of this curse.

With a grateful smile, Curtis left Mads in the wood-panelled room, making his way through the shop. He redialled Tim, the phone held between his shoulder and cheek as he unlatched the door.

"Hey man, lost track of time. I'll meet you in the parking lot behind the launderette in five."

Sliding the phone back into his jeans, Curtis found his eyes wandering back to the bone chime hanging innocuously by the door. It tinkled lightly despite there being no discernible breeze. Curtis shuddered and pulled the door closed behind him, hurrying back onto the street to meet his friend.

Chapter Nine

The final few hours at work seemed to drag by.

Curtis found himself checking the time far too frequently. The anticipation was clearly contagious because he caught Tim checking his own watch on more than one occasion.

As soon as the workday was finally done, Tim drove Curtis back into town to call on Mr Maddox again.

"You sure you don't want to come in with me?" Curtis asked as Tim pulled the truck into an empty parking space.

Tim grinned at his friend, still unsure how seriously to be taking all of this oddness. It was bad enough that his wife was into all the weird supernatural stuff without adding his best friend to the list too.

"Nah, man, you go ahead. I promised Angie I'd grab a few things from the store. Leave the keys in the visor just in case I finish up before you do. Good luck!"

Tim jumped out, closing the door behind him before taking off down the street.

Suddenly, Curtis felt his phone buzz in his pocket.

He slid it out and glanced at the display.

Unknown caller.

"Hello?" he answered.

There was silence on the line for a moment before a soft voice spoke.

"Is this the garbageman? Curtis?"

Curtis glanced at the phone in his hand uneasily.

"Yes. Who's this?" he asked with a frown.

Another stretch of silence passed before the caller let out a shaky sigh.

"It's Cathy."

Curtis's eyes widened, the phone almost slipping from his fingers in surprise.

"Cathy?? What the hell were—"

"I know. I know," she said, cutting across his outburst. "I'm so sorry, Curtis. After my realtor called, I tried to ignore everything, but honestly, the guilt has been eating me up."

Curtis could hear her sniffling and knew the woman on the other end of the line was crying softly.

"Why did you give it to me?" he asked, his tone less aggressive than it had been a moment ago. "Why me? And why no warning? You've literally ruined my life."

"I know." She wept. "I knew I had to pass it on and when I saw the garbage truck, I panicked and thought maybe it would be destroyed somehow. I won't lie; I knew there was a strong possibility that she'd attach herself to you, but I hoped she wouldn't get the chance. I was wrong and I am truly sorry."

Curtis laughed bitterly.

"If you're so sorry, then take it back," he spat. His emotions were getting the best of him, and he could feel his anger as it bubbled to the surface.

"I can't," said Cathy. She was openly weeping now. "I lived with that *thing* for weeks! I read every book and every article I could find online. I wanted to destroy that creature after what it did to Carla."

"Wait, who's Carla?" he asked.

"My sister."

Curtis heard her inhale deeply, then exhale in that distinctive way only smokers can. He pictured her, face wreathed in cigarette smoke. She probably looked much better than the last time he had laid eyes on her.

The thought brought his anger rising up his gorge like fire once more, but he swallowed it down with great effort. Cathy had finally sought him out. He needed to hear what she had to say.

"Carla had only returned home after a few months out travelling. She developed this crazy interest in all kinds of occult stuff when she was somewhere in Asia. But something happened that spooked her because one week she's telling me she won't be home until after summer, and the next week she's on the phone asking me to pick her up from the airport the following day.

"She wouldn't tell me what had made her change her mind so suddenly about continuing her travels. Next thing, this box shows up at her house. She wouldn't tell us who it was from, but the postage tags and stuff looked exotic, so we didn't wonder too much about it. From the moment it arrived, though, Carla changed.

"She became edgy, jumpy, and always seemed to be giving it the side-eye. Mom thought she'd gotten hooked on drugs or something, but I knew different. She's my sister. We've always been close. Always *were* close. I recognised what was behind her eyes and it was fear. She was terrified of something.

"Eventually, she opened up about what was happening and the woman in the box. I never saw her myself then, but one night, I stayed over at Carla's and when I woke up, I was covered in scratches. Anyway, Carla killed herself. Couldn't take it anymore so she sliced her wrists open in the bathtub."

Cathy sniffed and took another deep but shaky inhalation.

"I'm sorry about your sister," Curtis said quietly.

"You and me both," she replied. "I guess Carla thought I'd be able to figure it out because Mom found the box in her house addressed to me. She apologised in the note, and I honestly don't know to this day if she was apologising for killing herself or for what she was passing on to me.

"Mom dropped the box off and, well, I guess you know how things unfolded from there. I devoured everything I could find about possessed items and curses, even reached out to a few people online, but they were all clueless. They were clearly frauds looking for a quick buck and that's not what I needed. I tried throwing it out, tried burning it—"

"Me too," Curtis interjected.

"So you know this thing is fucking impossible to destroy. I saw some stuff online about giving away a curse. Basically, offering it to someone, and if they accept, the curse passes to them. Apparently, people in some parts of the world make good money 'taking' other people's curses. I wouldn't do it for all the money in the world. So, my choices seemed to be to kill myself or give it away.

"I'm gonna be honest with you, Curtis. I'm not the suicidal type. I love life. Always have. I stopped loving it when that bitch was haunting my every moment, but since I passed the box on, I'm loving life all over again. I'm sorry that I had to ruin yours to do it, but I won't take it back. It was nothing personal at all. Just know that."

"So I'm just stuck with it? You're just washing your hands of this shit?" Curtis asked angrily.

"I'm sorry, but yes. It's the only way I could reclaim my life. I know it's selfish, but that's life for you. Sometimes it sucks, and sometimes good people have to do shitty things to protect themselves. I suggest you do the same. Maybe find someone you don't like and pass it along. I don't know what to tell you, only that I can't help you."

The call disconnected.

Curtis stared at the screen in disbelief before hurling his phone across the truck. It bounced off the driver's side door and fell into the darkened footwell.

Curtis sighed heavily and pinched the bridge of his nose. He could feel a bitch of a tension headache brewing.

With another sigh, he reached across the truck to retrieve his phone. The call from Cathy had sucked the life right out of him, but he knew he still had plenty of reasons to be optimistic. Mr Maddox would have some answers and a way to rid himself of the creature from the box.

He stashed the keys under the visor and jumped from the truck. Mr Maddox's shop was only a few stores over from the parking space Tim had found, so the stroll was short. Looking around nervously first for any sign that the ghoul had followed him again, he took a deep breath and strode purposefully into the store.

The bone chime tinkled, announcing his entry and sending a shiver down his spine, and Mr Maddox's head popped up from behind a shelf near the back of the store.

"Ahhh, Curtis! Glad to see you back."

He smiled warmly and Curtis could feel his shoulders relax. If the man's presence alone could have that effect on him, then he was definitely optimistic about ridding himself of the box.

Mads gestured for him to follow, and as expected, Curtis found himself in the wood-panelled room again. The small man waved him to a wingback chair, stopping as he passed it to pluck a pile of books from its velvety seat. As Curtis lowered himself into the chair, Mads rested the books upon another already unsteady stack of tomes before plopping himself into a second velvety seat at the other side of the mahogany desk. He gazed at Curtis for a few moments from behind tented fingers as if contemplating his words before he spoke.

"I know that which haunts you," the old man said quietly.

Curtis had sat with his head bowed, pulling nervously at the skin around his nails, but now he lifted his head to meet Mads's eyes.

He proceeded to tell Curtis what he could of the creature in the box.

There were many of them, he said, with many different names, each entity attached to different receptacles for a myriad of reasons. He swept his hand along the glass wall behind him, not even turning to look at it.

Curtis found his eyes wandering along the case's contents again, wondering with a shudder what kind of horrible things existed in those boxes. Were they even more terrifying than the thing that currently resided in his apartment? More dangerous?

Mads continued.

Little was known about these types of creatures, but they always bore a curse of some kind that would afflict the person who came to be in possession of them, he told Curtis. They existed solely, it seemed, to bring terror and misery to their victims. They would bleed a person of their hopes and dreams, smother any relationships they had until they were completely isolated, and snuff out any chance of a joyous existence. Some will live quietly alongside their victim for many, many years, slowly siphoning away the very essence of whichever poor unfortunate they had latched on to. Others moved much more quickly and could evolve to become a very real danger to those around the victim. In the end, they all had the same effect, each one leaving a trail of desolation in their wake.

"Soul Eaters, I call them," said Mr Maddox solemnly. "Others in my line of work have their own names for these things. Light Eaters. Soul Vampires. One occultist I know in California calls them Demon Lampreys. You know, like those eel creatures? Don't let the romanticised names fool you, though, Curtis. These things are bad news."

There were only two ways to remove the curse.

The first was to gift the box to somebody else. The recipient did not need to explicitly know anything about the cursed box or that they were accepting ownership as such, but they did have to accept the receptacle willingly.

Curtis thought of his conversation with Cathy only moments earlier, then thought back to that day on the street last week. The day Cathy had handed him the box.

You have to say you'll take it, she had said.

The desperation in her voice, on her face.

Curtis winced, inwardly cursing the woman again for knowingly giving him the box.

How had her sister come to have the box? He wondered, and how long had Cathy held on to it before she couldn't cope with the ghoulish woman any longer? *Weeks*, she had said. She wanted it gone badly enough to pass a horrific curse on to a stranger.

Could Curtis himself pass it on?

No, he didn't think that he could. And certainly not to an innocent stranger.

Find someone you don't like and pass it along.

Cathy's words rang in his head. He mulled over all the relationships in his life, all the people he knew.

Sure, he'd had run-ins with some folk. Drunken disagreements in Broderick's, the occasional gripe with snarky customers along the garbage route. But Curtis didn't think he could bring himself to willingly inflict what he was experiencing upon anybody else.

"There is a second way to rid yourself of the box, but it's unimportant right now," said Mr Maddox. "It's very much a last resort, and I don't think we'll need to go that far."

Curtis listened intently to Mr Maddox as he pointed at some of the boxes behind the padlocked glass and summarised their contents. There was an amulet of sorts that he could create easily. The amulet was essentially a chain that should bind the wretched creature to the box. It was similar to how he had managed to come into possession of those already contained in his wall of boxes.

If the amulet worked, then Mr Maddox would take possession of the box and it would live indefinitely in the padlocked glass case behind his desk. If the amulet failed, well, things would probably become a whole lot worse for Curtis.

"The choice is entirely yours," Mads said gently. "If you need time to think on it, I completely understand. I have the amulet ready to go. It only needs a drop of your blood to activate it."

Curtis gaped at him. "My blood?" he asked incredulously.

"You are the one who possesses the box, so yes, only your blood will suffice."

"Pretty sure it's that damn box that possesses me," Curtis said bitterly. "Fine. Let's do this. I can't keep doing nothing, so if there's a chance that this will work, then I'm all for it."

Mr Maddox hopped from his chair, bustling around the room until he had all that he needed.

He unrolled a deep red parchment that looked as though it was made from the skin of an animal.

Oh God, I hope it's from an animal, Curtis thought to himself, his eyes widening as he watched the small man place an ornate dagger on the parchment. The overhead light winked off the steel blade, and Curtis gulped audibly.

Mr Maddox chuckled. "Don't worry, Curtis. It'll only be a little nick, just like in the movies. You'll see!"

He placed a small hessian bag on the desk and untied its opening. From it, he pulled what looked like a length of thin, silver chain. No fancy designs, no magical gemstones. Just a piece of chain like you'd pick up in any hardware store.

"I know what you're thinking," Mads said with a wink. "It *is* just a normal chain. It's the preparation I did earlier that makes it special. Most people would call it mumbo-jumbo, but that wall of boxes right there says otherwise. Now, hold out your hand, please. This might sting a little."

Curtis hissed as Mads nicked his palm with the fierce-looking blade. Instinctively, he tried to pull his hand back, but the old man held it in place above the chain, squeezing it into a fist. Curtis watched as a crimson rivulet snaked its way toward his wrist before beading and dropping to the chain below. As the fluid hit the chain, there was an almost imperceptible sizzling sound. Curtis gasped in wonder.

"Told you it's not mumbo-jumbo," said Mads with another wink.

He released Curtis's hand, and without removing his eyes from the chain on the parchment, he pushed a small first aid kit toward Curtis.

Curtis took it gratefully and rummaged through it until he found some alcohol wipes and a Band-Aid. As he tended to his wounded hand, he could hear Mads muttering beneath his breath, his eyes laser focused on the chain as he continued his incantation. A small red puff of smoke suddenly lifted from the parchment, and Mr Maddox sat back smiling, clearly pleased with his work.

"Now, you take this chain and when you get home, you put it across the top of the box. Doesn't need to be looped around or secured once it lies across the opening. That should prohibit the creature from escaping long enough for you to return here with the box. There are stronger spells and incantations I can use then to seal the box for good."

Curtis nodded eagerly, reaching for the chain.

Mr Maddox pulled the chain back from his reach and offered a warning. "Bind the box as soon as possible upon your return home. If you keep the chain in the vicinity of the box for too long without binding it, the creature will become aware of its presence and try to thwart your efforts."

He let the chain spill back into the hessian bag and held it out for Curtis to take.

"Do you have any questions before you leave?"

Curtis took the bag from the man's outstretched hand and nodded.

"Just one. Why do you always wait with your trash can? Is it because there are things related to curses and spells in there that you don't want anyone stealing or stumbling upon?"

Mr Maddox threw his head back and laughed, his robe rippling as his shoulders shook in amusement.

"I just enjoy the few moments of people-watching, Curtis." He laughed. "What would be the point in standing guard over a garbage can on the street with dangerous items in it, only for it all to be transported to the dump where anybody could get their hands on it?"

His eyes shone with mirth, his mouth twitching. But he was unable to keep the grin from splitting his face. Curtis, embarrassed as he was for not considering that, couldn't help but return the small man's grin.

They walked back through the store in silence, the weight of what was to come lying heavy on both of their minds. Curtis recounted his conversation with Cathy, Mr Maddox nodding as he spoke.

"Don't forget. Make your way back here with the box *tonight*," Mr Maddox whispered as he unlatched the door and pulled it open. "Good luck, Curtis!"

Curtis nodded and stepped out into the dying twilight. He remained deep in thought as he walked toward the parking lot to meet Tim. Not even the farewell tinkling of the bone chime could penetrate the tumult of his mind.

The ride back to his apartment had been unnaturally quiet. Tim hadn't probed too deeply about his meeting with the elusive Mr Maddox, and Curtis hadn't offered up too many details. He knew that his friend meant well, but also that he wasn't taking the situation too seriously. Hell, who could blame him?

Tim had made some light-hearted attempts at banter, but Curtis was a million miles away, locked inside his own head. His nerves burned with anticipation. If this thing worked, he could be free of the entity within hours!

The truck had barely come to a stop outside his building before Curtis had the door open, eager to get in and get the job done.

"You coming to Broderick's later for a few beers?" asked Tim.

Curtis hesitated.

"I'm not sure yet, man. It's been a heavy week. I'll give you a call in a bit if I'm feeling up to it."

"No worries, man," his friend replied. "If I don't see you later, don't forget the Spring Fling boat race is tomorrow afternoon. Bella made it clear that she expects Uncle Curt to be right there cheering her on!"

"Wouldn't miss it for the world." Curtis smiled, thinking fondly of the fervent concentration on the little girl's face as she had painstakingly painted her toy boat for the race the night he was supposed to stay over. He and Tim had watched from the deck, beer bottles in hand, as she had scrawled her name on the plastic hull, her tiny pink tongue poking from the corner of her mouth.

He shut the door and headed to the lobby, the music from Tim's truck increasing in volume as he gunned it back onto the road and headed for home.

The elevator doors were closed. Lifting his eyes, Curtis could see that it currently sat idle in the basement.

He hit the call button and stood back cautiously. A familiar distant groan signalled its ascent, and Curtis's stomach knotted and tensed as he watched the lobby button above the door light up a sickly yellow, reminiscent of cigarette smoke.

The metal doors whirred open, and darkness spilled out. His blood turned to ice as the shadows moved, a steady black form taking shape as the weak light from the lobby tried to hold back the night that spilled from within. The figure within the gloomy compartment stepped forward, and Curtis shrieked as a gnarled hand shot from the dark and clamped around his wrist.

Chapter Ten

"Jesus Christ, Mrs Mathers! Pardon my language, but you scared the shit out of me!" Curtis's hand rested against his chest, his heart still thudding against his ribs.

Mrs Mathers stood in the elevator doorway with a small wicker laundry basket resting on her hip, the Stygian void at her back.

"I'm so sorry, Curt. The lights went out right after the elevator door closed in the basement. I saw the lobby button light up, and honestly, I was a little scared myself. Didn't know who'd be waiting here when the doors opened," she said. "And please, call me Helena."

Curtis chuckled, amused at his own skittishness. Pulling his phone from his work pants, he swiped on the torch app and held the phone out to his neighbour. As Helena gratefully took the light source from him, he reached out and hoisted the basket from her hip.

Helena smiled up at him.

"Thank you, Curt. You're a good boy."

The pair winced as the elevator fluorescents suddenly burst to life, chasing away any lingering shadows and flooding the compartment with warm light. Helena cheered and Curtis grinned.

He stayed in the elevator until it reached the older woman's floor, then walked her to her apartment. As soon as she opened the door, the two small dogs ran to greet Curtis, sniffing and scratching around his legs. Helena took the basket from him and set it aside atop a nest of wooden tables inside the door.

"Coffee?" she asked.

Curtis reached down to scratch the fluffy black dog's ears while its spotty companion sniffed around his ankles, its tail a blur of motion.

"Not tonight, Mrs Mathers," he replied. "I'm just in from work, so I need to do a few things at home. Soon, though, for sure!"

"I didn't see Celia this morning?" Helena said, a question evident in her inflection.

"No, Celia is taking some well overdue holiday time," he said, thankful once more that he had remembered to contact the weekly cleaning lady.

Celia had been confused at the sudden request that she not come by for a few weeks. She had been concerned and questioned him incessantly about her standard of work and if it pleased him. He had assured her that she was a wonderful cleaner, but he had people visiting from out of town, so it seemed like the perfect time for her to take a few weeks' break. The white lie had slipped out easily, but it had put Celia's worries to rest and Curtis had no regrets in telling it.

Mrs Mathers hummed in approval, and they said their goodbyes, but as he turned to leave, Curtis had a thought.

"Mrs Mathers!" he called, turning back toward her door.

She pulled the door wide once more and grimaced at him.

"Sorry, Helena," he said sheepishly. "Is there any chance I could borrow your car for an hour or so tonight? I have a couple of errands to run back in town once I shower and change. If it's any trouble, I can just call a taxi."

Helena disappeared from the doorway for a brief moment before reappearing. She tossed a small bunch of keys to Curtis.

"How about you keep her for the weekend? All I ask is that you throw a little gas in her tank, and that you stop for a coffee Sunday when you bring back the keys."

Curtis grinned at his neighbour.

"I'll bring some cake to go with the coffee," he said, and Helena giggled in response.

Curtis bade Helena good night for the second time, then strolled back through the hallway to the elevator. The doors stood open, and the lights were still blazing.

Curtis found himself whistling as the lift descended smoothly to the fourth floor. He couldn't recall the name of the tune, but it was upbeat and catchy. He felt more positive than he had since it had all begun.

As he stepped from the elevator on his own floor, his whistling ceased.

He had serious business to attend to, hopefully for the last time. Now wasn't the time for frivolity. He walked to his apartment and gently opened the door.

All was quiet as Curtis padded silently around the apartment, flicking on lights and checking for signs of the dark-haired woman-creature.

He knew the light offered him no protection, but if he had to guess, it probably harked back to some childhood precondition.

Everyone knew that monsters lurked in the dark, hiding in shadows and tiptoeing through gloom. Light was the saviour of every scared child.

And every scared adult, too, it seemed.

As he stepped quietly down the hallway toward his bedroom, a sheen of perspiration dotted his brow. Curtis could hear the roar of his own blood rushing in his ears and the panicked thud-thud of his heart. It seemed so loud in the silence surrounding him that he almost felt as though his own body going through the motions was about to give him away.

As he neared his room, he could just about make out the box at the end of his bed.

The room was dark, the darkness softened only by a pale thread of moonlight that barely peeked through the clouds. The light of the moon did little to penetrate the shadows but softened the gloom enough to allow Curtis to discern one shape from the next.

As he stepped through the doorway, he pulled in a deep breath. Slowly, he pulled the length of chain from the hessian bag, tightening his fist around its cold links and offering up a silent prayer to any deity who wished to listen.

Curtis slapped the light switch, then dashed at the box, a primal scream assaulting his ears as he flung the chain across the opening. When the box didn't move nor the opening part, he realised the scream was coming from deep within his own chest. The deafening sound cut abruptly, and he was enveloped in silence once more, his ragged breathing the only thing to break the stillness.

His arms trembled slightly where he held the chain in place, and the slow realisation dawned on him that there was no movement from within. Not so much as a vibration.

It worked, he thought in amazement, his face splitting into a grin. *The goddamn magic chain worked!*

He gently removed his hands from the cardboard, stepping back quickly in case the thing in the box was trying to trick him and suddenly broke free. Curtis backed up slowly and quietly, his eyes never leaving the box.

But still, it did not move.

A triumphant laugh escaped his throat, growing louder and more jubilant with each passing second that the box remained closed and inanimate.

Curtis rummaged through his closet, rapidly pulling out a change of clothes, and headed to the bathroom to slough the sweat and stress from his body. As he left his bedroom, he pulled the door closed and clicked the lock into place. It really felt like he didn't need to, but after the week he'd had, he wasn't prepared to take any chances.

Not that the locks had made any difference before, he thought wryly, twisting the shower knob, the room slowly filling with steam.

Curtis pulled his grimy clothes from his lithe frame and stepped gratefully under the flowing water. As he lathered his body, he realised that he was humming that same upbeat tune again. A familiar feeling was beginning to flow through him. It was one that he wasn't accustomed to lately, and with a grin, Curtis recognised the warmth for what it was.

Happiness.

As Helena's old Toyota Camry rumbled along the road toward the town of Oak River, Curtis's eyes shifted once more to the cardboard box that sat benignly on the passenger seat beside him.

The safety belt was pulled across the box. It looked a little ridiculous, but he didn't care. The end was finally in sight and Curtis was taking no chances.

When he had returned to his bedroom, refreshed from both his shower and the injection of optimism, he had been pleased to find the box as he had left it. The chain still lay across the opening.

When he had gently lifted the box, the chain hadn't budged. Expecting it to slide off or move a little, he carefully carried it from the apartment, holding it close to him like a beloved child as the elevator carried them both to the lobby. Not once did the chain move.

Curtis pondered the magical chain in amazement as he gently strapped the box into the passenger seat of Helena's car before exiting the parking lot and heading for town.

The centre of Oak River was alive with people, but then again, it was a Friday night. Not to mention, it was Spring Fling weekend.

The colourful bunting that hung across the buildings on Main Street and looped lazily around streetlights lent the town a carnival atmosphere. The bright lights from the actual carnival were visible from the far end of the street, and as Curtis pulled into an empty parking spot close to the curiosities shop and opened the door, calliope music and cheerful shouts travelled gently on the crisp night breeze.

As he reached across to the passenger seat to remove the box, he heard a door opening a short distance away.

The hollow tinkling of the bone chime was all too familiar to him, and Curtis knew Mr Maddox had been watching for him, anticipating his arrival.

Pulling the box from the car, he bumped the door gently with his hip to close it, gripping the box tightly in one arm as he fumbled with Helena's keys. The car's lights flashed, and a chirruping noise sounded, assuring him that he had successfully secured his gracious neighbour's vehicle.

Mr Maddox stood almost entirely confined to the shadows of the shop's doorway. As Curtis drew nearer, the old man waved him in.

"You have the box!" Mr Maddox exclaimed, his head nodding enthusiastically as he eyed the cardboard container that Curtis carried almost reverently. "Great news, I had another visitor not long after you left. Patrick is an old acquaintance of mine and also very much experienced in these kinds of things. He likes to come and peruse my collection whenever he's in the area and compare it to his own. When he heard about your box, he wanted to stay and help me with the containment."

Mr Maddox closed the door, pulling the bolt into place, and Curtis shivered as the bone chime knocked gently. The main shop floor was gloomy but warm light spilled from the back of the store. He was more familiar with that part of the shop now and started in that direction. Mads shuffled along behind him, firing questions at him about how the evening had gone.

A tall white-haired man sat on the corner of the mahogany desk, leafing through a thick leatherbound book. He looked up as they entered and Mads introduced them both.

Patrick, or Paddy as he liked to be called, was a Spiritualist from a small town in rural Ireland. Paddy quickly recapped for Curtis how he had been born with a caul on his face, the seventh son of a seventh son. His family had known he would be spiritually gifted. Heck, the whole county had known, given the circumstances, he told Curtis. He had devoted his life to the same kinds of pursuits as Mr Maddox, and the two had crossed paths many a time before inevitably becoming good friends.

Curtis smiled and nodded at the man, a thousand questions racing through his mind. *What the hell was a caul?* Not to mention the seventh son of a seventh son thing. He thought that was only in movies and fantasy novels, but in hindsight, he had heard that the Irish had big families, so maybe it wasn't uncommon to be a seventh son or daughter over there. His mind still completely blown by the prospect of all the things these men had seen and dealt with. Things he couldn't possibly perceive.

Not knowing what else to do, Curtis held out the box. Mads gently lifted it onto the desktop, and the two men huddled over it, muttering and whispering, not necessarily to each other. Curtis stood quietly by the door, unsure of his place or what was expected of him now.

"So will I just head on out then?" he asked, his body already turning toward the doorway, eager to rid himself of the box and the terrible thing contained within it.

"Yes, yes," Paddy muttered in reply. "You're free to go now, young man."

Curtis exhaled heavily, relief blanketing him as he started for the door.

It was still early enough in the night to catch up with Tim at Broderick's for a beer. He felt like he deserved a beer or two after all he had dealt with in such a short time. Maybe he could decide on a plan of action and try to fix things with Lilah. Thoughts of her and of the future they could have together filled his mind and blurred his vision as he stumbled from the brightly lit room back toward the gloom of the shop.

"Curtis, wait!" called Mads.

His stomach dropped almost instantly, and as he whirled around to face the old man, he knew his features betrayed the cold fear that had reignited within him.

"Have you seen the creature this evening?" Mads asked, his voice tinged with urgency.

"The box is empty!" yelled Paddy, his gnarled features twisting in panic. "You've brought an empty receptacle. Have you seen her?"

"Yes," Curtis whispered, his eyes wide, as he watched the woman's soulless black eyes appear over Mads's shoulder.

Her eyes flicked from Mads to Patrick before coming to rest once again on Curtis. Her lips peeled back in a dreadful smile, her blackened gums and yellowing teeth fully visible. The smile stretched into a grin and then continued stretching to sickening proportions. As the thing's horrible mouth continued to widen unnaturally, its pallid skin in danger of tearing, Curtis's eyes widened in horror. His mouth dropped open, and he wanted nothing more than to scream at the two men to run for their lives, but all that escaped was a wheezing gasp.

Both men, recognising the sheer terror in the younger man's eyes, turned as one and came face to face with the creature from the box.

Mads shouted in surprise, but the woman whipped him aside, his head cracking against the wooden shelves and cutting off his yells abruptly.

Paddy shouted his friend's name, fear and anger marring his voice, but as she turned her hellish gaze on him, the old man's yells became shrieks.

Curtis watched in horror as she cupped the old man's face with both of her hands, her spindly, mottled fingers spread across his face in an almost tender fashion. But as Paddy's shrieks grew in intensity, followed quickly by rivulets of blood dripping down his face and beneath the collar of his shirt, Curtis knew there was no tender intention on the creature's part.

It knew what the men were capable of, and it intended to destroy them.

With a whimper, Curtis watched as the creature ran her thumbs up Paddy's face until she found his eye sockets. His screams ratcheted higher, and an unearthly growl rumbled from the woman's throat, followed by a wet popping sound. The ruins of the Irish man's eyeballs began to flow around her fingers and down his face, melding with the thin rivers of blood already marring his visage.

His stomach roiling, Curtis moved toward the door as quickly as his legs would carry him. Warm vomit erupted from his tightening stomach and landed on the floor in front of him in a steaming puddle. Strings of bile hung from his mouth, and he absently brushed at them with his forearm as he fled from the room.

Curtis slammed into the shop door and tugged at the handle, but it remained sealed.

He glanced back toward the lightened hallway that led to the back room, his eyes white and wide and flashing with fear. He could hear crashes and bangs interspersed with grunts and moans. Suddenly, Mads screamed. Another sickening crack was soon followed by silence until Paddy began to moan once more, his pained groans interspersed with broken fragments of long-forgotten prayers.

Whatever the thing was doing to the old man, it wasn't good.

His hands fumbled along the door in the gloom when the memory of the bolt latching into place slammed into him. *The bolt!*

With a mixture of terror and relief, Curtis reached up for the bolt. Behind him, the bone chime jingled tinnily, and the sudden realisation that there was no more noise coming from the back room made him freeze.

The silence around him was heavy and ominous. His breath shuddered as his fingers danced slowly and gently along the wooden frame, suddenly feeling the cool metal of the bolt beneath them. *Almost free.*

Curtis dared not move his head. He flicked his eyes, trying to use his peripheral vision to check for danger. He swallowed heavily, the click of his dry throat carrying like a crack of thunder in the deathly silent store.

A low, rumbling growl sounded right by his ear.

Ice flooded his veins, and tears pooled in his eyes.

In a flash, Curtis threw himself toward the door, his fingers drawing the bolt back at the same time. But before he could release the lock, he felt something close around his throat.

Panicked, he threw his hands up toward his neck, desperately pulling at the obstruction that bound him. His fingers scrabbled at string and feathers and smooth, hard shapes.

The bone chime.

The woman from the box was going to choke him to death with the bone chime!

Tears flowed freely down his cheeks as Curtis rasped and moaned. The string cut tighter into his neck with every jerky movement he made, and the thing's guttural growling filled his ears and echoed around his brain. As the already darkened room began to fade to full black, the last thing Curtis heard was the woman's hissing breath in his ear, her whispers lulling him into nothingness.

"Curtis. Mine."

Chapter Eleven

*M**ine.*

Curtis came to with a jerk, the mocking whispers still ringing in his ears. As the events of the previous night came rushing back at him like a runaway freight train, he spluttered and coughed. He winced at the flare of pain in his neck as he did so.

His throat felt raw and the delicate skin around his neck was on fire.

Rubbing gently at the area, he pulled himself into a seated position and dared to take in his surroundings.

Weak sunlight filtered through the posters and flyers littered around the glass door, doing little to penetrate the gloom of the shop. It was silent but the air felt heavy, and a metallic tang scented the room. As he stood, carefully assessing his body for any damage that might have been inflicted upon it, he surveyed the space around him.

The light that had spilled from the back room the previous night was still on, but now it flickered menacingly. As he started toward it, he stumbled over an array of goods that had been hurled from the shelves.

The floor was littered with broken glass in varying degrees of colour and size. Trinkets and odd-looking objects lay scattered among the debris pile, and everything was wet and shining from whatever liquids the glass bottles and jars had held. The cloying scent of oils, spices and fragrant herbs filled the air, but still, that coppery smell persisted beneath them all like a warning.

Curtis stepped around the broken things on the floor, and as he turned the corner, he froze, gagging at the sight before him.

A body lay on the floor, limbs splayed. The clothes it had worn were just tattered rags now and barely discernible among the blood and viscera that coated the body. Deep gouges marred the flesh, some in strange patterns, others as though a wild animal had unleashed its rage upon the poor unfortunate who lay there unmoving.

He inched closer, trying to identify which of the elderly men lay desecrated on the floor. Where hair had once flown from the scalp, it was now just an open oozing wound, the pulpy flesh of its cranial matter painted red to match the rest of the gruesome tableau.

Curtis could feel the hot tears that rolled down his cheeks, could hear the muffled sobs that came from his own chest, but somehow, he felt detached. Numb.

He knelt by the body with a grunt, careful to avoid the copious amounts of blood, when something caught his eye. He gently lifted the crucifix from the crimson neck and knew that it was Patrick who lay before him. The man had worn it proudly outside his collar, and it had caught Curtis's eye last night as it flashed in the light of the back room.

"I'm so sorry, Paddy," he whispered, gently placing the crucifix back on the old man's body. Curtis stood, looking toward the back of the shop where the light continued to flicker.

Was she still here?

Was he still in danger?
Was Mads dead too?

A thousand questions flitted through his detached mind and Curtis was certain he knew the answers to most.

He needed to get out of there and notify somebody. But how would he even begin to explain what had happened here?

Curtis knew the spotlight would be on him. As the pressure built and his mind began to fracture, he caught a glimpse of a future where he spent his days in a tiny cell, protesting his innocence. *She* would follow him there too.

Stuck in a confined space with her.

Mine.

He would be hers then. He didn't want to be hers. Curtis raced toward the door in a blind panic and flung back the bolt. As he wrenched the door open, the bone chime knocked behind him, and he cried out in fear.

But the bone chime hung innocuously where it always had, disturbed only by the breeze of the opening door, and if it held any stain of the evil that had wielded it last night, it showed no signs of it.

He pulled his eyes from the chime and turned to leave, almost falling over something that sat in the shadowed doorway of Mr Maddox's shop.

Curtis stooped down and picked up the box before stumbling out into the early morning light.

The brightly coloured bunting waved sedately in the gentle breeze. Most of the storefront windows and lampposts on Main Street were adorned with posters, each one announcing the table of events for the eagerly anticipated Spring Fling Weekend. The carnival, nestled into a large vacant lot at the end of the street, was quiet now, but in a couple of hours the air would be filled with the whoops and hollers of excited children. The fragrant smell of candyfloss and deep-fried delights would travel along the streets and alleys of Oak River, luring more festival-goers to seek out the thrills of the funfair. At the opposite end of the street, in the small town square, the bandstand had been decked out with even more bunting and bright bunches of balloons. Trestle tables had been set up beneath striped awnings and gazebos, some traders already setting up their stalls, hoping to catch the early visitors. The sky was a brilliant blue, with only the merest hint of cloud daring to mar what was shaping up to be a perfect spring day.

Curtis trudged slowly along the street, the box held in his grip. His eyes were deep pools of despair set into a blank face. His mind was a tumult of thoughts, none of which he could process as he glanced around Main Street like a frightened animal.

Soul Eater.

The town was slowly coming to life, even at this early hour, the playful pull of the festival weekend too much for some to ignore. Some of the business owners dotted the street, washing windows to a shiny gleam or shooting the breeze with passersby. Various members of the festival committee flitted back and forwards, straightening flags and picking up any stray articles of litter they had missed on the first go around.

A young woman sat alone outside the bakery, her head bowed as she scrolled through her phone. Curtis faltered to a stop a few steps from where she sat on the bakery's outdoor bistro seats, a tug-of-war raging in his mind.

I could just give her the box, he thought, *and be done with this whole nightmare. I don't know her; I'll never have to think about it again.*

His mind skimmed over thoughts of Cathy, and he understood her motivations now. He was a stranger to her. She chose him at random, sheer desperation to be rid of the box and its ghoulish inhabitant the only motivating factor in her decision. He felt a stirring of empathy for the woman and remembered how bereft she had sounded as she talked about her sister. And how the anguish had melted from her features when he had first taken the box from her. Oh, how naively innocent he had been, he thought bitterly.

He took another step toward the young woman, his arms already beginning to extend as if presenting the box as a fine prize indeed.

Sometimes good people have to do shitty things to protect themselves.

As he stepped closer, she lifted her face to him, her aquamarine eyes gazing at him quizzically. "Can I help you?" she asked.

"Yes," he croaked, "Could you take th—"

"Mommy! I got one with pink frosting!"

A small girl dashed through the open door of the bakery, waving her sugary treat at the young woman.

"Oh, baby, that looks delicious!" the woman exclaimed, smiling warmly at the little girl as she brushed aside blonde ringlets and crammed the cupcake in her mouth. The woman looked from her daughter back to Curtis, who still stood with the box partially extended toward her. "Do you need me to take that?" she asked him, assuming the man just wanted someone to watch his box while he went into the bakery himself.

Curtis pulled his arms back, hugging the box to his chest.

"No!" he exclaimed, backing up and moving a little further down the street.

His heart hammered in his chest as he widened the distance between his cursed self and the woman and child whose lives he could have changed irrevocably.

"Fuck!" he hissed to himself. "I could have ruined their lives! What the fuck is wrong with me?!"

Curtis walked in a daze along the street, berating himself. He spied an empty bench shadowed beneath the canopy of a massive old oak tree on the corner of Main Street. He dropped onto the wooden seat, exhaling heavily as he tried to figure out what his next move was. Across the street in the square, people bustled about with smiles on their faces and their whole lives ahead of them. Behind him, back in the curiosity shop, two men lay dead. Their only crime was helping a stranger.

Tears pricked at Curtis's eyes as the image of Patrick's mauled body flashed through his mind. He could have sworn he could still smell the sharp tang of the old man's blood in his nostrils.

Closing his eyes against the bright morning sunlight, Curtis tried to make sense of the tumult of emotions and thoughts that ran through his fractured mind. He tried to concentrate on the chirruping of the birds and the gentle murmur of the leaves above his head as they danced in the gentle breeze. Though the box on his lap felt light, he understood its true weight.

As he tried to plan his next move, a shadow fell across his closed lids, blocking out the sun. Curtis jolted, his eyes snapping open as a hand fell upon his shoulder.

Chapter Twelve

Lilah stood over him, her long golden hair hanging over her left shoulder in a thickly woven braid.

"Hey you," she said with a small smile, lowering herself onto the bench next to him.

"Lilah! I thought you'd left town," Curtis said. His heart fluttered in his chest like a caged bird as he drank in her presence. She looked great. Relaxed and happy, the edge of her white sundress fluttering gently as the breeze chased it.

"I was going to," she said, "but the girls talked me into hanging around at least until the Fling was over." She looked across to the square where more people had begun milling around, the sounds of happy laughter and idle chitchat travelling through the spring air. "I met Tim in Broderick's last night. Curtis, he's worried about you. *I'm* worried about you. He said you've been dealing with some stuff the past couple of weeks and that you won't talk about it."

Curtis glanced across at her.

"Don't believe everything Tim tells you," he said.

"Oh, really? So, when Tim tells me that I overreacted the other night and that you want me to hang around, should I just discount that?"

Curtis whirled on the bench to face her and caught the ghost of a smile tug at her lips as he did.

"Okay, fine, Tim is wise and all-knowing." He exhaled heavily. "Look, Lilah, I've never been as happy as I am when I'm with you. But there are some things going on, things you wouldn't believe if I told you."

Curtis lowered his head, but as he did, Lilah caught his chin with her fingers and pulled him toward her. She kissed him deeply.

"I love you, Curt. Whatever is going on, we can deal with it together. I don't care how crazy it sounds. I promise you. We need to cut the shit and just be honest with each other. Then we might have a chance at making a proper go of things this time. Do you want to grab a coffee? Maybe take a walk before the festivities are in full swing? If we nip this in the bud now, we could turn up to the Spring Fling together. Oak River's very own Sandy and Danny turning up to the end-of-year carnival at Rydell High." She smiled at him and kissed him again.

Curtis exhaled another deep breath and reached out, tucking a stray lock of golden hair behind her ear.

"Sounds like a great idea," he said, standing up.

Lilah stood too, and before Curtis could react, she was reaching for the box and pulling it from his grip.

"What's in here anyway?" she asked as she looked at the box with curiosity.

"It's nothing important," Curtis said, pulling the box away from her and tightening his grip on it.

Lilah gave him a funny look.

"Do you want me to take it? You can grab coffees?"

"No!" Curtis shouted.

Lilah took a step back, confusion and hurt casting a shadow over her delicate features.

Curtis groaned, cursing himself inwardly for his sudden overreaction.

"No. I mean, it's fine. I actually have to run home real quick. I borrowed Mrs Mathers' car to run some errands for her, so I'd better get everything back to her before I do anything else," he said, offering Lilah an apologetic smile as he began to turn slowly back toward Main Street.

"Okay," said Lilah in a small voice, her face filled with confusion. "I'll head over to the square and grab coffee while I wait. I'll come back to the bench here and wait for you. Don't be too long."

"Yep. Cool," said Curtis, although he was hardly listening at that point.

He turned and strode down Main Street with the box held tight to his chest. Lilah stood and watched him go, a puzzled look on her face but a glimmer of hope shining in her eyes.

Curtis was completely torn as he made his way back to Helena's Toyota. His heart was soaring with boundless joy at the prospect of fixing things with Lilah. It was all he wanted to do. But his head knew what the consequences would be. He wasn't willing to have Lilah become the next victim of the box.

He threw the box across to the passenger side of the Camry and hopped behind the wheel. The engine fired and he headed toward home, his body running on autopilot as his head and heart battled to the death, a showdown between love and logic where there could be no winners.

"Curtisss."

Curtis jumped, glancing across the car at the woman. The top half of her body, as far as her torso, was protruding from the box, and she was turned to face him. He could see the movement of her head in his peripheral vision as she swayed gently. She was like a cobra preparing to strike, but even more devastating and deadly.

"What do you want from me?!" he shouted, hating the fearful quaver in his voice. "Just leave me the fuck alone! Let me live in peace with Lilah." His voice broke as he spoke Lilah's name, a sob fighting its way up his throat.

The creature pulled forward until he could feel its hot, rancid breath in his ear.

"Lilahhh."

Curtis slammed his foot on the brake, and the car shuddered to a stop on the road. He turned to stare at the dreadful woman—the eater of souls—his hands clenched around the steering wheel so tightly his knuckles had turned white.

She stared right back at him, her features stretching into a horribly unnatural grin.

"Lilahhh. Mine."

A throaty chuckle began to crawl its way up the thing's neck, erupting into an ear-shattering howl of glee. It never took its dark eyes off Curtis.

He turned his head, seeing the apartment building in the near distance through the trees. He imagined bringing the box home. Bringing Lilah home. Putting her through the same torture he was currently living with.

Then he imagined himself without Lilah. No life to speak of because how could he possibly maintain any of his friendships and risk his loved ones becoming a target of the dreadful creature that now stared at him, silent once more?

And in that instant, Curtis knew what he had to do.

He put his foot on the gas, following the road through the trees instead of turning toward his building. The leafy canopy above cast the road in shadow, small shafts of sunlight filtering through the leaves to throw dappled light among the dark spaces.

Curtis lowered the windows, the rush of spring air invigorating him. The creature had disappeared back inside its cursed box and as the landscape whipped by, Curtis finally allowed the tears to fall unbidden.

He cried for himself and the unfortunate path that led him to the nightmarish box. He cried for Lilah and hoped her pain would heal quickly. He cried for Tim and his family. He hoped Bella followed her dreams as she grew older. He knew Tim and Angie would always encourage her to do just that.

He cried for the kids he'd never get to have himself.

Would he have had sons or daughters? Maybe both. Would they have looked like him or Lilah? Would they have been into rockets and nature like Bella?

Curtis was sobbing now, his vision blurred by a curtain of hot, stinging tears. But he knew where he was, the old pedestrian bridge just barely visible through the sheen of tears that marred his sight.

He hoped he was making the right decision.

The iron bench flashed by as the car crashed through the guardrail in a screech of twisted metal.

Guess the guard rail wasn't fit for purpose, Curtis thought idly to himself as the car plummeted from the cliff.

As the roar of the twisting river grew louder, a strangely calm sense of detachment enveloped Curtis. It would all be over soon. The box wouldn't be able to hurt anybody else or ruin any more lives.

Curtis closed his eyes and smiled.

Then everything went black.

Epilogue

The sun beat down on the town of Oak River.

The air was tinged with the warmth of spring, and the excited shouts and cries of children and adults alike carried along on the breeze and echoed through the town.

The Spring Fling festival was in full swing, and the town was alive with colour and sound. Flags flapped lazily and bright lengths of bunting were strung haphazardly from pole to pole.

The carnival was chock-full of people, the mechanical whoosh of the rides and tinkling arcade noises from the midway mingling in the air with the scent of fried foods and sweet candyfloss. Lights flashed and kids screamed as they were tossed around on rides that many would not have dared attempt if not for the goading cheers of their older siblings and friends.

Main Street was also bustling with families and friends as everyone made their way from the carnival to the festivities in the town square and back again, with many dipping in and out of the local businesses as they passed. All of the proprietors exchanged smiling pleasantries with their customers, even those who normally avoided the general public.

The small curiosity shop stood silent and dark, but nobody cared to notice.

Everyone was caught up in the fevered excitement of the Spring Fling.

The upbeat thrum of music from the bandstand filtered through the streets. A young man in a cowboy hat and snakeskin boots crooned soulfully about his "Achy Breaky Heart," and a crowd had gathered before the stage. On one side, line dancers moved in practised formation as they stomped and slapped their way around the beat. Next to them were random groups of old and young alike as they moved to the music in their own rhythmic way.

People had brought fold-out chairs and picnic blankets, and the onlookers sat between the bandstand and the stalls, their hawkish eyes and tapping feet taking everything in all at once.

Mothers nursed tiny babies as they chatted with friends, and toddlers held spongey biscuits in their chubby fists as they cooed and clapped, oblivious to the party atmosphere. Older kids charged among the crowds, chasing each other with childish laughter and wild abandon. Teenage couples held hands beneath picnic tables where parents couldn't see, as grown-up couples kissed each other openly, giggling into each other's shoulders. Across from the square, a bench beneath the shade of a huge, old oak tree sat empty. Two coffee cups lay abandoned beneath its seat: one empty, one full, and both cold.

A couple of elderly gentlemen concentrated fiercely as they challenged one another in a game of chess. Both wore their Sunday best even though it was Saturday. Behind the men sat a bench full of elderly women. Some held knitting needles, with bags of wool set between their sensible shoes. Another held the local paper and read titbits of gossip out loud for the others to hear. A particularly juicy piece of local news drew gasps and crows of laughter from the small group.

Behind the bandstand, accompanied by parents and grandparents, aunts and older siblings, gaggles of children moved along the grassy track that led to the sandy bank of the Oak River itself. Here, in the heart of town, the river meandered easily alongside the low banks, having cascaded its way down from the clifftops farther away.

Every year, the Spring Fling committee held the annual boat race. All the kids in town were encouraged to build or buy their own boats and the results were usually hilariously unusual.

The race was due to start soon and most of the kids milling around were testing the nautical abilities of their creations before it was time to hit the starting line farther downstream.

Among the tall reeds that protruded in straggly clumps from the shallow edge of the river, a small girl waded a little higher upstream.

The water lapped at the ankles of her scuffed yellow boots as she swept a new clump of reeds aside in search of her boat.

Her daddy had helped her to release the boat farther upstream, where the banks were quieter. They had watched, enthralled, as the little boat was pulled downstream by the current. It never wavered or toppled, and then it had rounded the bend where her daddy had said it would be caught in the reeds. They had trudged back along the grassy bank and when they reached the reedy part of the river, he urged her into the water to search. He stood watching the little girl, tall, solid, and safe, as she stepped daintily into the crisp water to hunt for her boat.

His phone chimed its familiar ringtone and right before he answered, he called to her to watch her footing and not to venture out beyond the reeds.

She rolled her eyes. How dumb did Daddy think she was?

The girl felt guilty then because she knew her daddy was distracted. He had tried to call her uncle a ton of times this morning and she didn't think he'd gotten through. It was probably her uncle on the phone right now, looking to see where they were and where he could meet them for the best view of the boat race.

She pushed her small hands into a big clump of reeds, close to where the water began to get deeper and move faster. She balanced herself carefully. It wouldn't do to tumble head over heels into the river. Her mom would make them all drive home to change her clothes and she'd miss the race!

The girl smiled radiantly as her fingers brushed against the solid mass of her boat. She grasped at it, but it was tangled in the reeds. Moving closer but still moving carefully, she parted the reeds with her arms and untangled the boat with deft fingers. She could still hear her daddy on the phone nearby. He sounded agitated and the girl chewed her lip absentmindedly as she worried about her daddy, her uncle, and the boat race.

Something else lay wedged behind the reeds.

She could make out its bulky shape as it bobbed and nudged against the clumps of vegetation. Looping her belt around the boat to keep it secure, she delved a little further into the reeds, curiosity getting the better of her innocent mind.

It was a box.

The box was made of cardboard, and although it was wet, the structure seemed perfectly sound. It must have been carried downstream only recently.

She carefully tugged the box closer before lifting it gently from the river. It was light, like it was empty.

She peered closer at the strange stickers and symbols on its surface, then lifted the flap to peek inside.

The box was empty except for a few strands of dark string or hair on the very bottom.

With a shrug of her shoulders and a small smile, the girl whispered to the box, "You're mine now."

It was the perfect size for carrying her boat after the race and any other odds and ends she might come across during the festival. Daddy had promised to win her at least three stuffed animals at the carnival. What better way to cart her prizes around than in this perfectly usable box?

As she splashed her way from the shallow water to the grassy bank, the bright spring sunshine reflected off her auburn hair, casting her in a fiery glow.

She heard her daddy finish his call as she stepped from the river.

"Bella!" he called. "We gotta go. Did you find your boat?"

"Yes, Daddy," Bella replied, smiling sweetly. "And I found a neat box, too, to keep all my stuff in!"

"That's great, sweetie," Tim replied. He didn't look back at his daughter, only held out a hand for her to grasp. "I'm gonna have to leave for a little bit right after the race. I need to go look for Uncle Curtis and see where he's got to."

"Okay, Daddy," replied Bella.

She ran on small legs to catch up to him, hugging the box closely to her chest. Today was gonna be the best day. Bella just knew it.

Acknowledgements

Well, here we are. I never thought I'd be writing the acknowledgments for my own book. Eeek!

First and foremost, I want to thank you the reader, because without you this book wouldn't have been born. I'm a writer sure, but I'm a reader first, and as someone who straddles both sides of the line, I know how difficult the process is, and how heavily we rely on reader support. Interacting with us online, reaching out to us, reading our books and leaving reviews and/or recommendations means the world and makes all the hard work worthwhile. The reader relies on the writer to provide escape from the daily grind. The writer relies on the reader to carry their stories like a song on the wind. It's a symbiotic relationship. We need each other. We appreciate each other. So thank you from the bottom of my cold, black heart.

My ever-suffering love Wig (yes, there is a story behind the nickname, and no, he doesn't wear a wig), without you there to push me, support me, and celebrate every little win, I never would have made it. This win is as much yours as it is mine.

My beautiful boys, Kyran and Odhran, you didn't help at all. In fact, I'd probably have finished sooner without you. But without you both, the horror would bleed from the pages of my work and darken my world unbearably. I love you both more than words can ever say and I promise not to use either of you as bait when the zombie apocalypse inevitably comes.

My mother, Frances, didn't do anything either, but she's the best person I know and she deserves a mention. Without her, there would be no me, and to be fair, she has always encouraged my daydreams and allowed me to wear the 'family weirdo' badge with pride.

My sisters Casey and Shauna who, although they hate horror, will occasionally give me ideas. Some day, I'll write you both into a book. Whether you survive or not remains to be seen.

Dayna and Conor, who spent many a drunken night listening to me bang on about books and writing and horror and blah blah blah... I love you both dearly.

Then there are the writers. My peers who saw the desire I had to get the words on paper and offered a helping hand, words of encouragement and advice, and an understanding ear when I needed to vent. Imposter syndrome is a real monster, and these guys were always there with a flashlight in the dark to chase that monster away and help me to believe in myself:

Ben Young, who answered my incessant questioning with warmth and kindness every single time. Ben is awesome.

Patrick McNulty, who was the first to believe in me enough to offer me an outlet for my writing. I would never have made it this far without him.

Jim Ody, who gave me advice, answered questions and sometimes just checked in on how I was doing. Writing is a very solitary craft, but he made sure I was never truly alone.

Phil Baker, without whom I would never have figured out the correct way to write dialogue! Phil is another who has been with me from the beginning, always ready with advice and encouragement.

There are so many more of my fellow writers that I could easily add to this list, but we're in danger of these acknowledgements becoming the sequel to the book so I will offer love and gratitude here to them all. If you have ever offered me advice or support, if you have ever cheered me on from the side-lines, just know that it means so much to me, and I will always hold each and every one of you close to my heart.

My editor, Danielle Yeager, who polished my story into something fit for human consumption. My cover designer, Christy Aldridge, who put up with my indecisiveness and worked her magic to deliver something that matched what I had in my mind exactly.

My wonderful beta and arc readers deserve a lot of love too! Thank you for taking a chance on me!

The Books of Horror community on Facebook also deserves a huge shout out! Hands down the best place on the internet. We all share a love of the dark things in the world, but only offer each other kindness and support. And book recommendations.

Aaaaallllll the book recommendations.

Tiffany Koplin is a goddess among mortals. How she keeps everyone in line is one of life's great mysteries. RJ Roles, who created the greatness that is BOH and was also the first person to publish my work. Few feelings come close to holding my words in an actual book, and for that I will be forever grateful for him.

And finally, THANK YOU again, for making it the whole way through my acknowledgements. My excitement got the better of me. Can you imagine what my speech would be like if I ever won an Oscar??! Yikes!

About the Author

Leigh was born and raised in the beautiful garden county of Wicklow, Ireland. She is the mother and proud protector of two wonderful boys, a black Labrador, and a three-legged cat that hates people. She is also the bane of her long-suffering partner James' life. Leigh has a fierce love for all things morbid and macabre. She is an advocate for mental health, having struggled with her own demons for many years. They're not quite friends yet, but there's definitely some kind of truce in place. She cites Ronald Malfi, Kealan Patrick Burke, and of course, Stephen King, as her most favoured authors and sources of inspiration.

Cursed is Leigh's debut book, and though she hides it well, she is very proud of herself.

You can find out more about Leigh's work and any upcoming releases on her Instagram and Facebook pages: LeighKennyWrites

Lets be friends!

Got social media?

Sure you do.

There's no escaping it these days.

Lets be friends!

You can find me, follow me and... wait.. this is getting a little weird now, isn't it?

Come support me, find out about upcoming releases, or even just say hi on Facebook and Instagram:

Leigh Kenny Writes

See you there!

www.ingramcontent.com/pod-product-compliance
Ingram Content Group UK Ltd.
Pitfield, Milton Keynes, MK11 3LW, UK
UKHW032013300125
454444UK00004B/93